Blake gave a laugh of unbridled amusement.

'Your generosity embarrasses me, Mistress Blair. Indeed it does.'

His amusement irked Katherine somewhat, but she continued to smile softly. 'I would not have believed a man of your phlegmatic character capable of embarrassment, my lord,' she said with a hint of sarcasm.

'By that I take it that you mean I am not easily excitable—dispassionate, even.' His eyes narrowed and glittered meaningfully and his voice softened. 'Oh, come now—after what occurred between us the last time we found ourselves alone together, I think you know me better than that.'

Helen Dickson was born and still lives in South Yorkshire with her husband and two sons on a busy arable farm where she combines writing with keeping a chaotic farmhouse. An incurable romantic, she writes for pleasure, owing much of her inspiration to the beauty of the countryside. She enjoys reading and music; history has always captivated her, and she likes travel and visiting ancient buildings.

Recent titles by the same author:

MASTER OF TAMASEE
HONOUR BOUND

KATHERINE

Helen Dickson

MILLS & BOON

All the characters in this book have no existence outside the
imagination of the author, and have no relation whatsoever to anyone
bearing the same name or names. They are not even distantly inspired
by any individual known or unknown to the author, and all the
incidents are pure invention.

MILLS & BOON, the Rose Device and
LEGACY OF LOVE are trademarks of the publisher.
Harlequin Mills & Boon Limited,
Eton House, 18–24 Paradise Road, Richmond, Surrey TW9 1SR

© Helen Dickson 1996

ISBN 0 263 79599 3

Set in 10½ on 12½ pt Linotron Times
04-9606-71107

Typeset in Great Britain by CentraCet, Cambridge
Printed in Great Britain by
BPC Paperbacks Ltd

CHAPTER ONE

ON THIS day in March, 1641, Katherine Blair had particular reason to feel happy, for it was her nineteenth birthday and already a hint of spring was in the air.

Her face was lovely and serene, her skin smooth and as white as magnolia and she was humming softly as she busied herself with her needlework. Seated by the window she made a pretty picture, with the sunlight streaming through the latticed panes, giving the room a soft warmth and bringing out the richness in the wood of the carved oak chests and cupboards, the depth of colour in the tapestries which lined the walls and the burgundy brocade hangings of the canopied bed.

Often her gaze would stray out of the window of Ludgrove Hall, a large Tudor mansion pleasantly situated on the banks of the Avon, close to the city of Warwick, and home of the noble Russell family. It was a quiet, gabled manor house, surrounded by walled courtyards and gardens. The Russell coat of arms stared out of every room—modelled in plaster over the chimney-pieces or embroidered on hangings and cushions. On the death of her father, Thomas Blair, eight years ago, Katherine had come to live at Ludgrove Hall as her Aunt Harriet's ward.

Katherine raised her head when her cousin Matilda came in, her round face flushed and grey eyes wide. As always Matilda, an exact replica of her mother in face and form but, thankfully, not in character, was overdressed. Katherine felt sorry for her. Matilda had forever been in awe of her mother, who always insisted that her daughter look her best. It was imperative that she made a good impression at all times—her future depended on it.

In Katherine's opinion, all the ribbons and frills only succeeded in making her look ridiculous but, out of consideration for her cousin's tender feelings, Katherine would never dream of telling her this.

'Mother wishes to see you, Katherine,' Matilda said breathlessly, having run up the stairs too quickly in her eagerness to do her mother's bidding.

A summons to her Aunt Harriet's presence was enough to cause Katherine some alarm. Putting her needlework aside, she rose. 'Do you know why, Matilda?'

Matilda shook her head. 'No, but Sir George Carrington has just left. He's been with Mother for the past hour or more. Maybe it has something to do with him.'

'No—I think not. You must be mistaken. Why should Sir George's visit possibly concern me? How did your mother look? Angry?'

'As well you know, Katherine, one can never tell

with Mother. If you don't mind, I'll wait here in your room until you return,' she said with some agitation, twisting her hands in front of her, a habit which always irritated and angered her mother. As Katherine hastily tidied her hair, pushing the stray rebellious golden locks behind her ears, she thought anyone would think Matilda was the one being summoned to the sanctum.

But Katherine was fond of Matilda, who was a year younger than she was. Matilda and Henry, who was away at his studies at Oxford, were her cousins, her Aunt Harriet's children to Lord Russell, a widower prior to this marriage, who had two children from his previous marriage, Blake and Amelia.

Smoothing her skirts with trembling fingers, Katherine hurried along the gallery which ran along the entire first floor of the house. A shaft of late afternoon sunlight pierced the leaded windows and shone on the fine portraits of the Russell family, the great men and women of the past who lined the walls on either side of the gallery.

She moved down the wide oak staircase, wondering as she went what she had done now. She ran through her mind any misdemeanour serious enough to give her Aunt Harriet cause to summon her to her presence immediately. Had she forgotten to visit one of the sick on the estate the other day when her aunt had been unable to do her weekly round of good deeds, ministering to the sick and needy, and had ordered her to go instead? No, she thought, that could not be it.

Matilda, with her astute and methodical mind, had been with her. She would have made sure that no one was missed. Katherine had not been out walking or riding unattended either, so that could not be the reason. Perhaps she had been seen talking too long to Sir George Carrington's house guest, the handsome Lord Forbes, when he had waylaid her in the church porch after the service last Sunday. But he had approached her and it would have been impolite of her to ignore him.

Confident that her conscience was clear, unable to think of anything she had done which was serious enough to warrant a reprimand, she knocked on the door of her aunt's sitting-room, a room few entered unless summoned.

Ever since Katherine had come to live at Ludgrove Hall, she had been painfully aware of her aunt's continued dislike. She had only taken her in because, on the death of Katherine's father, Aunt Harriet's brother, she had considered it her duty to do so.

Katherine had been allowed to live as a member of the Russell family, sharing Matilda's lessons, learning all the manners and customs of the household, in the hope of one day making a suitable marriage. Aunt Harriet did not ask for gratitude—but she expected it, nevertheless.

Katherine considered her aunt a hard, unfeeling

woman, who showed little love for her children. As to her suitability as a wife; only Lord Russell could put an answer to that. But there was no escaping the fact that he had begun spending a great deal of his time in London, having become more involved with the running of the family shipping company started by his father.

The Western Trading Company was a highly profitable mercantile company and becoming increasingly so as more of the West Indian islands and the American mainland passed into British hands. Lord Russell had employed others to do the work; his oldest son, Blake, having left the Navy, had captained one of the vessels, trading commodities across the Atlantic.

However, at this time the country had been in a state of depression, for which the Crown had to take much of the blame. Many London merchants had been suffering infringement of charter rights and heavy losses. It was a time when Lord Russell had considered his presence was required in London to oversee the running of the Company—much to his wife's chagrin. She had thought his time would be best spent at Ludgrove Hall to oversee the upbringing of his children and to run the estate, instead of leaving it all to herself and a bailiff.

Harriet was tall and statuesque, and still a handsome woman though in her late forties. Her round, strong-jawed face, enhanced by her dark eyes and fine arched brows, still bespoke some of the beauty which had once captured the attention of Lord Russell.

She had been a Blair prior to her marriage. The Blairs, an authentic, if sadly decayed family, their roots firmly embedded in the north of the country, belonged to the old English aristocracy. Despite the loss of their estates and their subsequent financial distress, Lord Russell, on the death of his first wife, had deemed it an honour to marry into such an old and distinguished family.

Katherine was aware of her aunt's deep displeasure, as Harriet observed her from across her small writing desk. In her aunt's opinion, she lacked humility and was considered wilful and stubborn with a tempestuous nature and a reluctance to conform. This was due, her aunt believed, to the fact that she had inherited bad blood from her mother—a Roman Catholic—who was never mentioned in the Russell household.

It had been with great reluctance that her aunt had taken her in, making her her ward, but thankfully her father, who had been an astute and shrewd businessman, had succeeded in acquiring immense wealth, having risen by his own good fortune and endeavours. On his death, all was left to Katherine, ensuring she would be eagerly sought after in marriage.

'So—here you are,' Harriet exclaimed, watching Katherine advance towards her. 'I told Matilda to fetch you immediately.'

'I came straight away, Aunt.'

Harriet gave her one of her dangerous looks, believing she scented sarcasm. 'Don't be impertinent, Katherine,' she snapped.

Katherine resented her aunt's tyranny towards her, but open conflict between them was rare. Better to endure, she thought sensibly, than make life too unpleasant for herself at Ludgrove Hall.

'I've just had a visit from Sir George Carrington,' her aunt went on, her eyes taking on a sudden gleam, as if in triumph. 'No doubt you saw him leave?'

'No, Aunt. I was employed at my needlework.'

'Such a charming man—don't you agree?'

'Yes,' Katherine replied, wanting to disagree but knowing better than to do so, wondering where this was leading. Something was definitely afoot and she did not like the feel of it. Ever since she had reached the age of eighteen, a year ago, she had been aware of her aunt's increasingly anxious efforts to find a husband for her.

Always being one to come straight to the point, her aunt did just that. 'I have decided on a match for you, Katherine. Sir George has asked for your hand in marriage and I have accepted on your behalf. Consider yourself fortunate.'

Katherine stared at her. All the colour drained out of her face. 'Fortunate? Sir George? No, Aunt. You cannot mean that. I cannot marry Sir George. Why—he—he is so *old*.'

'Old? I do not consider fifty old. Sir George is a

fine figure of a man still—and by no means too old
to sire children. He is a good catch for any woman, I
would say. He has long shown an interest in you,
Katherine. You must be aware of that?'

The only thing Katherine was aware of was that
Sir George was eager for money and Lord Russell
eager to acquire more land—which Sir George had
plenty of. How valuable a union between two families of substance could be, she thought bitterly.

'I suspect it is my inheritance Sir George is
interested in, Aunt, not I.'

Although her aunt's expression remained hard
and inscrutable, she could not deny that what her
niece said was true. Katherine's inheritance was
enough to tempt any man.

'Gracious, what ails you, Katherine? Sir George
could have the pick of any girl in the district but he
chose you. Why—you should be down on your knees
in gratitude that he should show interest in you at
all.'

'I do not feel gratitude, Aunt. I am obliged to Sir
George for his interest but I must refuse his offer of
marriage.'

Her aunt's face hardened and her lips became set
in a thin line; she had half expected this reaction
from her niece.

Katherine knew that her aunt would not be beaten
on this; if she succeeded in marrying her off to Sir
George, then her problems where Katherine was
concerned would be at an end. She would be able to

concentrate on finding a suitable match for Matilda, who would no longer be overshadowed by her beauty. Unlike Katherine, Matilda was more biddable by nature and had a quiet demeanour; while ever Katherine remained on the scene, Matilda stood little chance of acquiring a husband. Her aunt's lips parted from their compressed line.

'You are too stubborn, Katherine, too wilful by far. When you are married to Sir George, it will, no doubt, cure you of these tendencies.'

Katherine smiled wryly. 'Then all the more reason for me not to marry Sir George, Aunt. Not only is it my inheritance he covets but he sees me as someone to be a mother to his brood of six children. Why—his oldest daughter Mary is almost as old as myself.'

'Nevertheless, you will get over your aversion. I doubt Sir George will bother you overmuch. At every opportunity he will be away in London.'

'Spending my inheritance at the tables, I don't doubt,' said Katherine dryly. 'I have heard that Sir George's family fortunes are in decay, that he is an inveterate gambler and has taken to drink and low company. No, Aunt. I don't want to marry him. I won't marry him,' she said defiantly.

Katherine saw the muscles of her aunt's neck quiver and her face go white with anger at her disobedience, but she stood and faced her, unflinching beneath her hard gaze.

'You should know better than to listen to gossip, Katherine, for that is all it is—exaggerated gossip put about by idle tongues with nothing better to do. However—I find your manner singularly tiresome,' she said icily, 'and your behaviour unmannerly—and the pleasure it gives you to thwart my every wish conveys to me your ingratitude. I shudder to think what your father would think of you now.'

Memories of her beloved father, dead these eight years, caused Katherine's eyes momentarily to cloud with sorrow, and the sensitivity that was so rarely shown to the world softened her lovely face. Her early years with her father at their home in Rochester in Kent—the town where he had chosen to live after the loss of his family's estate in the north of England—had been particularly happy ones; it was perhaps for this reason that the shock of being reminded of him was all the greater. She blinked tears from her eyes.

'I don't mean to seem ungrateful, Aunt, and if you think so then I do beg your pardon, but if I were to marry Sir George then I would be an unwilling bride. My father would not have wished that for me. I will not give myself to any man I do not love.'

Lowering her eyes, she thought achingly of the one man to whom she would give her very soul— how she *longed* to see Blake. This longing that tore at her heart was more profound than Sir George's obsession that she became his wife. But the love she carried for Blake was hopeless, for when he had last been in England one year ago he had not come to Ludgrove Hall but had gone instead to Oxfordshire and become betrothed to Lady Margaret Tawney, the beautiful daughter of the Earl of Rockley.

Her aunt stared at her as if she had taken leave of her senses. With her chin thrust out her face became ugly with scorn.

'Love? What has love to do with anything? Marriages in families such as ours are made for gain, not love. Sir George's fortunes may be somewhat depleted but he comes from a family rich in lineage, with an estate to equal our own.

'You are nothing but a girl with little to do other than let your mind dwell on idle fancies. I will not have it. Do not try my patience further, Katherine. Now—go to your room and let there be no more talk of your refusing to marry Sir George. It is all arranged. You will be married within the month and that is final.'

Sparing herself just enough time to go to her room and explain hurriedly to Matilda what had transpired between her aunt and herself, and desperate to concentrate her thoughts on what could be done, Katherine left the house in a helpless rage, heedless of the biting cold wind penetrating the vents in her clothing. After passing beneath the high stone archway of the gatehouse, she took the path leading her away from the house and the nearby village of Appleby.

She headed in the direction of the open countryside, uncaring that her aunt would be furious that she had dared to disobey her and not returned to her room as ordered, but had fled the house to walk the countryside unattended. This very act of defiance gave Katherine a fierce sense of satisfaction, an action she knew she would have to pay dearly for when she returned to the house.

Her situation seemed hopeless—to be trapped like this when life was beginning to hold such promise. In two years' time she would be of age, independent of her Aunt Harriet, free to do what she wanted with her life. But her aunt couldn't wait to marry her off. If only she had someone to fight her cause in the house.

Lord Russell, with his kindly manner, would have provided a sympathetic ear, but he was in London. Amelia—whom Katherine had missed dreadfully since her prestigious marriage to the Earl of Landale last summer—who had little affection for her stepmother, would have championed her cause and encouraged her to rebel. But she resided in London with her husband, where her life had become one long round of gay excitement at the Court of King Charles and his French wife, Henrietta Maria. There was no time to appeal to either.

Lost in thought, Katherine was unaware of Lord Forbes until he reined his horse beside her. Dismounting, he courteously removed his wide-brimmed hat adorned with soft white plumes.

'Why,' he smiled, 'Mistress Blair. It is most unwise to be out walking alone.'

Katherine looked at him, slightly taken aback by his sudden appearance. Lord Forbes was Sir George Carrington's house guest and, when she had first been introduced to him, she had treated him as she would any other young man. In fact, his expression of perpetual boredom had irked her somewhat. But as she had got to know him better, her feelings had undergone a subtle change and she had been flattered by his attentions—although he stirred nothing very deep inside her.

Rowland Forbes was young, in his early twenties, of slender build, slightly taller than Katherine, and with fair wavy hair falling to his shoulders. His face was handsome enough, though marred by his slightly prominent eyes and a faint sulkiness to his full mouth. Had Katherine looked a little deeper into his character she would have seen that, beneath his elegant exterior, his manners and his aristocratic affectations, he possessed a ruthlessness which would stop at nothing.

'Why, Lord Forbes,' Katherine breathed. 'Forgive me if I seemed startled, but you took me quite by surprise.'

'Then I apologise most sincerely. But why so downcast, Mistress Blair?' His eyes narrowed and he smiled teasingly, knowingly. 'No—don't tell me,' he laughed. 'But could it possibly have something to do with Sir George's proposal of marriage?'

Katherine's eyes flew to his. 'You know of this?'

He nodded. 'Aye. Sir George did speak of it. I

take it that by your despondency you are not
enamoured of marriage to Sir George?'

'I most certainly am not. The mere thought of
such a thing appals me.' She sighed almost despair-
ingly. 'The problem is—how to get out of it. Aunt
Harriet is determined that I shall marry him before
the month is out.'

'Can she make you?'

'Yes. Since I became her ward on the death of my
father—and until I am of age—she has complete
control over me. Sadly, there is no one I can appeal
to.'

'Not even Lord Russell?'

'No. Lord Russell is in London.'

'I see.' He sighed, replacing his hat. 'I also in a
day or so.'

'Oh? You are to leave Appleby?'

'That is so. I have been Sir George's guest for the
past four weeks and, pleasing though it has been,' he
said with a wicked twinkle in his eye as he looked at
her, 'tomorrow I must depart for London.'

As he was about to climb back onto his horse, on
impulse, Katherine reached out and placed her hand
on his arm.

'Wait—please.'

Lord Forbes turned and looked at her.

'How—how are you to travel to London?'

'Sir George is to send his carriage to London to
fetch his daughter home. She has been staying with
friends. He has kindly offered me the use of it.'

Katherine looked at him with new interest; already, the semblance of a plan was beginning to form in her mind. This was better than she had dared hope for. At the prospect of escape from her Aunt Harriet and marriage to Sir George, her heart began to beat fast and she felt a great sense of excitement.

'Lord Forbes—will you take me with you?' she asked, the words tumbling out of her mouth.

Lord Forbes stared at her askance.

'Oh—please—do say you will. There is no one else who can help me.'

'But—but—Mistress Blair, what you are suggesting is highly improper.'

Katherine gazed up at him imploringly. 'I don't care. Please take me with you.'

'But—London. Where will you go?'

'To Amelia. She is my aunt's stepdaughter and married to the Earl of Landale. I know she'll let me stay with her a while. Please—you cannot refuse me this.' The request came straight from her heart.

'But what you are asking is reckless in the extreme, Mistress Blair. What of your reputation? Have you not thought of that?'

'I care little for my reputation—it is small price to pay to escape marriage to Sir George. Besides, even with my reputation ruined, I shall still have my inheritance.'

The mention of her inheritance caused Lord Forbes to look at her sharply. 'Which will go to your husband on your marriage, naturally?'

'Yes. Or, failing that, to myself when I become twenty-one.'

Lord Forbes became thoughtful as he appeared to consider her request, but he had already made up his mind to take her with him. Rowland Forbes had an inbuilt instinct for self-preservation—always quick to grasp an opportunity. The mention of Mistress Blair's inheritance had swayed him, for when his father had died he had left him with a rundown estate in Hereford and a pile of debts.

The only way out that he could see—and being born to the ease of life as an aristocrat—was for him to marry an heiress. And here was the delightful Mistress Blair, almost offering herself to him. How could he possibly refuse her request? By the time they reached London he would have made sure that she would be so compromised that she would have no choice but to marry him.

A ruthless gleam appeared in his eyes and he was hardly able to conceal the excitement he felt. Allowing nothing of his thoughts to show, he nodded slowly.

'Very well, Mistress Blair. I shall escort you to London if that is what you wish. But—you do realise the position you place me in, do you not? It is hardly the way for me to repay Sir George's hospitality by carrying off the lady he hoped to marry. If he should discover what I have done, there is every chance that he will call me out. You must take care to tell no one of what you intend, otherwise,' he said with faint amusement—and more truth behind his words than Katherine realised, 'your Aunt Harriet may insist upon you marrying me instead of Sir George.'

Katherine flushed scarlet at his words for, indeed, this was something she had not considered. 'Oh— you need not worry, Lord Forbes. I shall make quite certain that no one learns of my intention to leave— or how, on reaching London, I happened to arrive there.'

'Good. Then meet me at Appleby Lane End tomorrow afternoon at three o'clock. It is a quiet enough spot. I shall tell the coach driver to expect another passenger. Cover your face to avoid recognition.'

As Katherine made her way back to Ludgrove Hall, perhaps she would not have felt so elated had she seen the ruthless gleam in his eyes and his lips set in a savage grin of satisfaction that fate had dealt favourably with him at last, and realised that she had played right into Lord Forbes's hands.

Stretching out his long booted legs in front of him, well satisfied after his meal of pigeon pie and vegetables, with bread cut from a giant loaf on a wooden trencher, Blake Russell relaxed on the high-backed settle to one side of a glowing sea-coal fire, his hand resting on the handle of a pewter tankard foaming with fresh brewed ale.

As he sat, he correctly gave the impression of being a tall man and strongly built. Everything he did was controlled and sure. His hair was of sable blackness, thick and with a hint of curl to it, falling to his shoulders. His eyes were so deep a brown as to be almost black and his skin the colour of bronze, burnt by the tropical winds and sun.

He sat in the shadow of the overhanging eaves of the wainscoted room of the black-and-white timbered coaching inn where he was to stay the night, along with others *en route* for London or the west country. The room was full of occupants, most of them dining. Blake was to travel on to Ludgrove Hall at first light.

In mellow mood his thoughts turned to his father and of how sudden his death had been. Why, he had scarcely had time to moor his vessel at the Pool below London Bridge, having just returned from the West Indies, when Amelia had sent word for him to go at once to her home where his father had been taken critically ill. Unfortunately, and sadly, he had died before Blake had time to get there.

Frowning and intent, Blake thought of the changes this would make to his own life, for there would be little time for adventuring. Now he must settle down to the humdrum life at Ludgrove Hall and the running of the trading company in London. Still, the thought of his betrothed, the fair Margaret, awaiting his return at Rockley Hall in Oxfordshire, and their impending marriage did much to compensate.

Margaret was the sister of Rupert Tawney, a good friend of his. Blake had been at school with Rupert, and it was Rupert who had introduced him to Margaret. She was fair and sweet, with all the right attributes a man could wish for in a wife, but the Navy and, later, his journeying to and from the Indies had kept them apart. Now that his father was dead and the shipping company belonged to him, he saw no reason why their marriage could not go ahead.

But there was no denying that he was more at home on water, feeling the heaving of the ship's deck beneath his feet, than on dry land. Dear Lord, how he would miss that, he thought with regret. No more sailing the ships—the great mobile fortresses embattled against piracy and storm—to Barbados, Antigua or the American mainland, acquiring cargoes of tobacco, indigo or cotton.

How he would miss the familiar shipboard smells of hemp and pitch, the feel of the savage, burning sun on his face and of seeing the white sands shimmering in the heat as the sun blazed down mercilessly out of a sky bluer than England had ever seen.

Swallowing his ale, his thoughts turned to Ludgrove Hall and his stepmother. How would she take the news of her husband's death? he wondered. Amelia was to bring his body back to Appleby for interment two days hence. He had come on ahead to break the news.

At a sudden rush of cold air he glanced towards the door, his gaze taking in a young couple who had just entered. The room was crowded but the landlord made room for them at a small table. It was the woman who held Blake's idle attention. She was shrouded in a cape, the hood pulled over her head putting her face in shadow. She was quite tall and moved with a regal grace, causing more heads to lift momentarily from their food and stare in curiosity. Blake watched her sit down at the table, her back towards him as she faced the young man she was with. He noticed how long and slender her fingers were when she raised her hands and removed the hood of her cape covering her hair.

The sight his eyes then beheld was so unexpected that it caused his breath to catch in his throat. The soft light from the oil lamp above shone fully on her, lighting her hair, the colour of burnished gold, with an unearthly brilliance, like a living flame, glorious and bright, shining like a beacon in the darkness of a moonless night on a black sea. He relaxed, content to let his eyes dwell on that glorious mass.

It held him entranced as he watched the light play on its changing colours as she moved her head while she ate and chatted to her companion. Only once had he seen hair that colour but, devil take it, he couldn't for the life of him remember where. Ladies had always been an important feature in his life and there were few who could resist his charms when he had had the time and chose to exert them. Most he had dallied with, he remembered—but this one?

With hair that colour? If he had known her intimately, then how could he forget?

Having finished eating, the young woman stood up and appeared to bid her companion goodnight. By her very manner Blake suspected that she was not his wife. Then she turned, the light falling fully on her face.

At that moment he recognised her, remembering in a rush where he had seen hair that colour before. He was dumbfounded. For a moment he thought fatigue had produced some kind of hallucination— surely this lovely young woman could not be his stepmother's niece, Katherine Blair? It was two years since he had last seen her and she was much changed, no longer an adolescent girl but a stunningly beautiful young woman.

'Good Lord,' he breathed. 'Who would have thought it?'

But what the devil was she doing here? With narrowed eyes his attention became focused suspiciously on her companion. He was of youthful appearance, his features somewhat pale and delicate, but being a man of the world Blake's experienced eye told him the type of man he was. The Court of King Charles was rife with men such as he.

CHAPTER TWO

KATHERINE did not see Blake in the shadow of the room, sitting motionless, watching as she moved away and climbed the stairs. What was Mistress Blair doing here? he asked himself. Alone and with a man who was unknown to him—what game was this? Again he fixed the young man with his full attention, anger beginning to stir against him and Mistress Blair, for it was plain to him that something was afoot. After a while the young man rose with a conspiratorial smile and a wink at the innkeeper. Blake watched him disappear up the stairs and, certain of his intent, gave him no more than a minute before he, too, rose and climbed the stairs.

But it was a minute too long. The terrible truth of Lord Forbes's scurrilous intent had dawned on Katherine and, too late, she realised her mistake in putting her trust in him. What a *fool* she had been. She had brought this upon herself, had been duped like the green girl she was. Panic sprang to life inside her as Lord Forbes advanced towards her, a steely glint in his pale eyes.

Having already divested herself of her gown, she felt particularly naked and vulnerable. She had never been close to a man before—never been kissed or caressed. These were things she had dreamt of happening to her with Blake—but things did not always turn out as they did in dreams. It had been foolish to hope that Blake might notice her one day. However, she had not envisaged that her first experience of love would be like this—forced upon her against her will. She shrank back and began to tremble as Lord Forbes approached her, his hands outstretched, and he laughed, a particularly piercing laugh, which plucked at her taut nerves.

'Please, Lord Forbes, leave my room this instant. I did not invite you in.'

Not discouraged, he moved closer still. 'No? Oh, come now, Mistress Blair, do not tell me you're going to be difficult. I do not think I misread the signals. For someone who cares so little for her reputation, one night of love will not go amiss. Why—you're trembling,' he said softly.

'It is hardly surprising,' replied Katherine crisply.

Lord Forbes's hand closed over her arm and, drawing her towards him, his fingers reached up and gripped her bare shoulders, making her tremble more than ever. However hard she struggled to escape, his vicelike grip was relentless.

Held captive against him, Katherine saw the slackness of his lips and the fire in his eyes as his face descended on hers. Utterly revolted, she turned her head to avoid his mouth, letting out a shrill cry of desperation. It was this desperate cry that alerted

Blake to the chamber she was in and, without hesitation, he flung open the door.

At Blake's sudden appearance Lord Forbes spun round, reacting angrily.

'Sir—kindly leave,' he ordered. 'You are not welcome.'

Ignoring the request, Blake moved into the room, a murderous expression on his face, his eyes flashing dangerously. Lord Forbes released his grip on Katherine who stumbled back, as startled as he was by the arrival of this man looming in the doorway like an angry, avenging God. At first she did not recognise the tall figure, so relieved was she that rescue had come, in whatever form.

It was only when he moved further into the light that she recognised those darkly handsome features that were so dear to her heart. He was just as she remembered, his mouth large and firm with a hint of flashing white teeth beneath his slightly parted lips. His jaw was square and strong but it was his eyes that held her. In the dim light of the chamber they looked black, with mocking lights dancing in their depths.

Katherine found the whole of him vaguely disturbing and frightening—in fact, there was something almost satanical about his presence. She stared at him, rendered speechless. Her mouth formed his name but no sound came. For one brief moment she forgot her predicament and looked at him with loving eyes, her heart beating with the unbelievable joy and comfort of knowing he was there. His face was tanned, and with his presence the contours of the room were swept away, replaced by the wide blue seas that washed the shores of the faraway lands he had frequented.

But now she was filled with shame and humiliation that he should find her in such sordid circumstances. She wanted to die. She felt weak and lost as his eyes raked over her with disgust or contempt—what matter which? Unable to meet those accusing angry eyes, in her anguish and self-consciousness she lowered her lashes.

Only for an instant did Blake's expression betray what he felt upon seeing Katherine, who did not see his face quicken or the admiration which shone fleetingly in his eyes. Her eyes were the colour of a tropical sky, he thought, as blue as blue could be, her mouth full and soft. Why had he never noticed how lovely she was before? But when he had last seen her she had been no more than seventeen years old and, to him, still a child.

He was overcome with anger at himself, for so readily falling victim to her charms, which he directed against her and the man she was with. Had he not enough to deal with at this time with his father's death without Mistress Blair creating an outrageous scandal? Curse the wench, he thought angrily, for her foolishness and thoughtless stupidity. He glanced at Lord Forbes, his murderous rage cooling to ice-cold anger, and the iron control his military training had taught him to employ came to his aid as he looked with freezing contempt from one to the other.

Katherine shrank back beneath the look that Blake fastened on her, and she was aware of the anger he must feel at finding her in such a compromising situation. A man such as he, with a hard inflexible will, would never understand the situation, for she knew how her conduct must look to him.

Having no idea who Blake was, who had intruded on what had promised to be a night of unbridled passion, Lord Forbes continued to glare at him.

'I asked you to leave, sir,' he repeated angrily. 'Can't you see that the lady and I wish to be alone? You are in the wrong chamber. Kindly find the innkeeper and ask him to direct you to your own. You have no place here.'

Blake arched his dark brows. 'I am by no means lost,' he said, speaking slowly, each word enunciated, making quite sure this stranger understood all he had to say, 'and when you say I have no place here then you are mistaken. You see, I am Lord Russell of Ludgrove Hall. The lady you have so compromised is my stepmother's niece—and while ever she resides in my house and is under age, then she is under my care and protection. What was your intention, pray? To seduce her or rape her? I must say that what I witnessed when I entered the room was no gentle seduction of an innocent maid.'

Lord Forbes gaped at him, at first too astonished

to speak. His face had gone quite grey. He looked at Katherine, swallowing nervously.

'Is this true? Is he who he says?'

Katherine shook her head. 'No,' she said, having regained some of her composure, angry that Blake, as he always used to, had succeeded in making her feel foolish. 'This gentleman is Blake Russell, Lord Russell's son. Ludgrove Hall is his father's house and I will only be answerable to him.'

'My father is dead,' Blake threw at her coldly. 'I am on my way to Ludgrove Hall to break the news to his widow—your aunt.'

Katherine stared at him in bewilderment, swamped with remorse at this terrible, unexpected news, for she had been truly fond of Lord Russell. She lowered her head, close to tears.

'I—I am so very sorry. I—I did not know.'

'How could you?' said Blake, knowing how much she had cared for his father and that he should have chosen a more private moment to break the news to her, but he was too angry to pay court to Mistress Blair's tender feelings. His cold brown eyes continued to look at her without emotion. 'Amelia is to accompany his body back to Ludgrove Hall two days hence.' He turned his attention once again to Lord Forbes. 'Kindly enlighten me as to your identity, sir?'

'Of course,' gulped Lord Forbes, an ambarrassed flush at being caught out like this spreading over his face. 'I am Lord Forbes of Swinburn Manor in Hereford.'

Blake nodded. 'Ah—yes, I have heard of your family,' he said, understanding at last what the knave was about. This man's father had been unable to resist the rattling of the dice box or the smile of an accommodating whore, had squandered his entire fortune, and had left his son with nothing but a pile of debts and a dilapidated heap of stones in Hereford. By all accounts this son was of the same ilk.

Little wonder he had set his sights on Mistress Blair, seeing in her a means of paying off some of his debts—or creating more—whatever the case. 'Were your intentions honourable,' he went on, 'then you would have paid court to Mistress Blair in the usual manner, but by your actions I am made all too well aware of your intentions and am right to suspect that your motives regarding her are dishonourable.'

The words were delivered in a cold and lethal voice which caused Lord Forbes's face to pale. 'You—you are mistaken, sir,' he stammered, 'and if that did prove to be the situation then I would be prepared to marry Mistress Blair. Indeed—I would be honoured to do so.'

'How gallant of you,' Blake growled sarcastically, 'and I'm sure you would be. I am aware of the dire straits you find yourself in since the death of your father. Having made an accurate assessment of your situation, I do not think I would be far from the truth when I say that, being aware of Mistress Blair's inheritance—which is quite substantial, I believe— you intended to place her in an impossible situation—to compromise her in such a way—thus ensuring that she would have no choice but to marry you. Correct me if I am mistaken.'

Lord Forbes gave a nervous, almost apologetic laugh, aware that Lord Russell had made him look a hapless fool. 'Sir—that was not my intention,' he lied. 'Mistress Blair asked me to take her to London—begged me, in fact. I—I thought—'

'What? That by doing so she was asking you to seduce her?'

'No—I—'

'Save your excuses, Lord Forbes. The hour is late. I would be grateful if you would delay your departure for London until I have spoken to you in the morning—when I shall leave for Ludgrove Hall— taking Mistress Blair with me. Now leave us. I wish to speak with her alone.'

Lord Forbes did not need telling again. Blake Russell's reputation was such that he knew better than to stay and argue. With immense relief he quickly made his escape.

Blake watched him go with contempt before turning to Katherine. Still in her state of semi-undress, she held her head high, in defiance of Blake's forthcoming anger, making no attempt to cover herself. Perhaps now he would notice her, would see that she was no longer a child.

Ever since she had set eyes on him when he had been an arrogant sturdy youth, she had come under his spell. Being ten years older than she, he had always kept himself aloof, spending much of his time away from home in the Navy—and over the last few years sailing to and from the West Indies in charge of one of his father's merchant ships. In between times he had paid court to Lady Margaret Tawney, which had torn at Katherine's heart.

No one had ever guessed at the emotion the sight of Blake or the mere mention of his name always aroused in Katherine. Not Matilda or Amelia. Not anyone. She did understand that he must be deeply saddened by the tragedy of losing his father and deeply regretted that in running away from Ludgrove Hall she had only succeeded in adding to his troubles.

Blake came to stand over her, seeing her lips tremble, her hair a wild tangle tumbling about her shoulders. In her struggle with Lord Forbes her breasts had almost sprung free from the bodice of her petticoat. Reaching out, he picked her cloak up from where it was lying on the bed and handed it to her.

'Here—cover yourself,' he ordered harshly, for he found it extremely disconcerting speaking to her while she was in this state of undress. If she had been anyone else, and at any other time, he would have let his eyes feast with pleasure on this tantalising vision of loveliness. But she was his stepmother's niece and, by all accounts, the cause of so much disruption at Ludgrove Hall of late. The only feeling he could allow himself where she was concerned was anger, for by her own fault she had brought about an impossible situation at a sad and difficult time.

But there was no denying that he was disturbed by the recollection of the graceful figure she had presented before wrapping her cloak about her nakedness. For a brief moment he felt a sharp pang of regret and uncertainty that he was betrothed to Margaret for Mistress Blair had suddenly and unexpectedly presented herself to him as an ideal candidate for a wife.

Like Margaret, she was fair, with blue eyes, and equally as wealthy, but there the similarity ended, for by nature they were entirely the opposite. Margaret had a sweet and gentle disposition, not the fiery, volatile nature of Mistress Blair. Whoever married her would have to curb her spirit, otherwise she would lead him a merry dance.

'Well? I am waiting for an explanation,' he demanded harshly, angry with himself for letting his thoughts run on in this way. 'What have you to say for yourself? Are you aware of what would have happened had I not seen you below and followed you up here?'

By the very coldness of the voice with which he addressed her, Katherine felt the full force of his anger. Drawing her cloak tightly about her, she turned from his accusing eyes. She would have to tell him the truth. He would find out anyway when he reached Ludgrove Hall—and how else could her presence here with Lord Forbes be accounted for?

'I was running away from Ludgrove Hall,' she said softly.

'Running away? Why would you wish to run away? Have my family not given you all the care and consideration you could have desired since coming to live at Ludgrove Hall?'

'Oh, yes—of course,' she replied, turning to face him, 'and I do not mean to seem ungrateful.' She sighed deeply. 'In truth, it was my aunt I was running away from. She has arranged a match for me, you see.'

'By your actions one you do not find agreeable, I take it? Who is the unfortunate fellow?' he asked dryly.

'Sir George Carrington.'

Her answer was such as to cause Blake some amazement, but he gave no indication of this. 'Oh, I see. And what is wrong with that? Sir George is a fine man. You should be grateful,' he said, echoing her aunt's words. But, as he said this, he could not explain the relief he felt, knowing that she had disobeyed her aunt. It was the first time he had ever condoned her defiance, which surprised him.

Now, looking at her with fresh eyes, at her glorious coloured golden hair and extraordinary looks, he could not help feeling that such perfect beauty would be sadly wasted on Sir George Carrington.

'I will not marry him.'

'What is your aversion to Sir George?' asked Blake.

'His age—and—among other things, I dislike him exceedingly.'

Blake gave her an enquiring look. 'So—I take it that you would prefer it to be an affair of the heart when you marry?'

'Yes. I will marry for love—nothing less,' she replied, meeting his eyes steadily, wishing she could tell him all that was in her heart.

Blake cocked an eyebrow with wry amusement and mastered a faint smile. 'Love! My dear Mistress Blair—how naïve you are. People rarely marry for love.'

'Oh, but you are wrong, my lord,' she said passionately. 'What of Amelia? Did she not love the Earl of Landale?'

On reflection, Blake nodded slowly. 'Aye, I suppose Amelia loved him well enough,' but he failed to add that the Earl of Landale had been more attracted by the generous dowry Amelia had brought him—that his love for her had been only lukewarm.

'And—and then there is yourself, my lord,' she dared to venture hesitantly. 'Are you not marrying the Lady Margaret for love?'

Blake looked at her steadily for a long moment before replying, 'Lady Margaret is all I could want in a wife. We understand each other. She is gentle and pure and loves me well enough.'

'There you are, then,' said Katherine, her heart twisting painfully at his reply—although he had failed to say that he loved Margaret in return. 'No power on earth will force me to marry Sir George Carrington.'

'You may not have to. I doubt even Sir George will have you when he learns of this. I understand that you asked Lord Forbes to take you to London. Where had you a mind to stay?'

'With Amelia.'

Blake nodded, relieved to learn that she had not been eloping with Lord Forbes after all. 'Then your efforts would have been in vain. Not wishing to bring about our displeasure, my sister would have sent you back to Ludgrove Hall in humiliation. You are under our care until you are of age. I would advise you to remember that, should you have a mind to run away again.'

He turned from her and went to the door. 'I shall see about securing a carriage for the morning. Be prepared to leave at first light.' He removed the key from the lock and held it up. 'Should Lord Forbes decide to come seeking you the moment my back is turned, I shall make quite sure he gets no further than the door. Goodnight, Mistress Blair.'

Katherine watched him go—so formal, so terse, for there was a time when he had addressed her as Katherine. His departure, followed by a click of the key turning in the lock, brought burning anger to her cheeks. How dared he lock the door? How dared he lock her in as one would a naughty child?

After a while, her anger abated and she sank onto the bed, her thoughts turning to Blake's father. Her heart was heavy with his loss and what it would mean to her life at Ludgrove Hall. One consolation was that Blake would be present more often— although she suspected that his marriage to Lady Margaret would now soon take place.

Going to seek his own chamber, Blake's thoughts were travelling along the same lines, triggered by the change he had found in Katherine. Because of his father's death he was having to think seriously about spending more of his time running the estate. He was returning to Ludgrove Hall as the new Lord Russell and intended to establish new rules. Blake had found a letter delivered to his father from his wife two weeks ago, complaining bitterly of her niece's conduct. After this latest escapade of hers, it seemed high time that leniency was replaced by more positive action. No longer would her defiance be overlooked—he intended to be obeyed.

The following morning it came as no surprise to Blake to discover that Lord Forbes had left the inn before dawn in an attempt to avoid meeting him. Unperturbed by this, and having secured a carriage, he took a subdued Katherine back to Ludgrove Hall in deep disgrace. Her disappearance with Lord

Forbes had been found out and had shocked and scandalised the whole household.

Katherine had not been as discreet as she had thought on leaving Ludgrove Hall. One of the servants had seen her slipping out furtively by a back entrance to the house and had reported it to her Aunt Harriet. She had also been observed waiting at Appleby Lane End and climbing into Sir George Carrington's carriage. On enquiry, it had soon been established that Katherine had run off with Lord Forbes.

Scandal such as this had travelled swiftly. By the following morning, Katherine's disappearance had been talked about all over Appleby. People loved a scandal and had gathered in clusters to whisper, and some to laugh, with malicious pleasure, while others in the higher ranks of Appleby society had been shocked and outraged that, after providing a roof over her head, Katherine Blair had ungratefully repaid her aunt's generosity by running off with a scoundrel.

By the time Blake deposited her in the hall of Ludgrove Hall, its woodwork gleaming and with the familiar smell of lemon polish and beeswax, the whole house was a-buzz with her fall from grace. But another subject of conversation would soon temporarily overshadow Katherine's escapade—when the death of Lord Russell was announced, the whole of Appleby would be plunged into mourning a man they had both loved and respected.

For Katherine, it took a great deal of courage to step out of the carriage. She paused, tired and despondent, almost too afraid to enter the house. An air of quiet hung over the great building, as if it already knew of its master's demise. She wanted to turn and run back to the carriage rather than enter through those huge oak doors and face her aunt's wrath. As though he read her mind, Blake's hand closed firmly over her arm.

'Come, Mistress Blair,' he said harshly. 'Don't tell me your courage has deserted you?'

The words gave a jolt to Katherine's heart. Lifting her chin she set her jaw indignantly, narrowing her eyes in anger as she fixed them on his.

'My courage is as intact now as it was when I left this house yesterday, my lord.' Wrenching her arm from his grasp, she moved ahead of him through the great double doors, which had been opened by one of the household servants. Behind her, admiration flickered briefly in Blake's eyes for the way she squared her narrow shoulders in a determined effort to meet her adversary head on—like a soldier going into battle, he thought.

It was cold in the hall, despite the fire blazing in the huge iron grate which threw tall, grim shadows up the grey stone walls. The journey back to Ludgrove Hall had seemed interminable to Katherine. She had struggled against an overwhelming desire to fill the silence between herself and Blake, but his stony profile had been enough to prohibit any suggestion of conversation between them. Physically he was so near to her but mentally so far away.

'I do not wish you to speak to Matilda until I've broken the news to her about our father,' said Blake. 'You will go to your room, where you will remain until either myself or your aunt send for you.'

Katherine's eyes flashed rebelliously for just an instant, but Blake threw her a hard warning look, his expression one of seriousness and impatience, reminding her that this was not the time for a display of pique. Lowering her lashes, Katherine nodded.

'Very well,' she uttered meekly.

At that moment there was a flurry of skirts and a pattering of slippered feet on the wooden boards of the stairs. Looking up, they saw Matilda, holding her skirts up in both hands so as to allow her to move more quickly. Her cheeks were aglow as she ran across the hall, such was her delight in seeing Katherine back.

'Katherine!' she exclaimed joyfully. 'How glad I am to see you back. . .' but there she faltered as Blake stepped forward. 'And Blake.' With a squeal of sheer delight she flung herself at him, wrapping her arms about his neck and pressing her cheek to his. Like everyone else at Ludgrove Hall, it was two years since last she had seen her half-brother of whom she was especially fond.

Watching their fond reunion, pain twisted Katherine's heart. How she wished she could be accorded the same intimacy whenever she met Blake.

When Matilda stood back, her eyes were full of bewilderment as she looked from one to the other, wondering how they had come to arrive together.

'I cannot believe that you are both here. But— but, Blake—how did you come to find Katherine? And Katherine—why—I thought—we all thought. . .' she stammered before falling silent with embarrassment.

Blake's face was set hard as he looked at Katherine whilst addressing his sister. 'Let us say our paths just happened to cross,' he said dryly, causing Katherine to lower her eyes at the memory of their meeting. 'Where is your mother?'

'In her sitting-room. She is in a rare temper because of Katherine's disappearance,' Matilda said, casting Katherine a nervous look.

'Aye—I don't doubt,' growled Blake.

'Perhaps I should go and see her and explain,' offered Katherine tentatively.

'No—better not. Now is hardly the time. I will see her first. If she is as angry as I suspect, then you will only succeed in enraging her further. Go to your room and wait until you are sent for,' Blake said in a tone which made Katherine stiffen. 'You, too, Matilda,' he said gravely. 'There is a serious matter I have to speak to your mother about. I will speak to you shortly.'

Alarm filled Matilda's eyes. 'Why—what is it?

Blake, what has happened? Please tell me? It is
something terrible—I sense it. Tell me now?'

Blake's whole expression softened, as it always
did whenever Matilda was distressed. 'Not until I've
seen your mother,' he said gently.

'Oh, very well. If you insist,' she said with a sigh.
'But—can't I stay with Katherine until you've seen
her?'

'No.' The harshness returned to his voice.
'Mistress Blair will go to her own room and await
the outcome of my meeting with your mother.'

Downcast, her shoulders drooping, Matilda pro-
ceeded to climb the stairs.

'You, too, Mistress Blair,' said Blake. 'I will send
word to you shortly.'

His manner caused Katherine's cheeks to flush
with burning colour and anger once again to stir in
her breast. His look was one she had learned to
detest for it was the same one he had often used
when she had first come to live at Ludgrove Hall—
quelling—a look an adult would give a cross and
troublesome child.

'Do not make yourself my gaoler, my lord. I am
not a child.'

'No? How old are you, Mistress Blair?'

'Nineteen.'

'Ah,' he sighed. 'And still an incorrigible child. Tis
worse than I thought.'

'I am not to be dismissed and sent to my room
because I have misbehaved. I shall go to my room

because it pleases me to do so and to be free of your odious company.'

Her outburst caused Blake's black brows to draw together dangerously. 'I see. Well—because of your infantile behaviour, Mistress Blair, it seems that I must treat you like a child. However much you dislike me, you will be seeing a lot of me from now on—so you will have to endure me with the best grace you can. And while you live in my house I will be spoken to with respect.

'It might have escaped your attention, but I have the unenviable task of informing your aunt that her husband is dead. I am seriously concerned of the effect his demise will have on every member of this family. I find your attitude ungracious. If you thought so little of my father after he gave you a roof over your head when you needed it most, then 'twill serve us all if you are out of sight. I doubt very much that your aunt will wish to be bothered with the embarrassment your foolish escapade has caused her at this present time. She will be too distressed.'

His voice was so harsh that Katherine started, but there was something about his expression that caused her to step back, not offended. She was not insensitive and did understand the strain he was under; she should have known better than to provoke his anger. Beneath his burning gaze she lowered her eyes, immediately contrite.

'Yes—of course. Forgive my thoughtlessness—my insensitivity. Despite what you think I was truly fond of your father and shall miss him terribly. I did not mean to seem ungracious.'

Looking at her quiet face as she was about to turn from him, Blake found himself touched by the sadness in her lovely eyes. Had he not had his father's death to deal with, he would have seen that none of this was easy for her either. By her own naïvety and foolishness she had brought her situation upon herself and would doubtless have to suffer the consequences of her actions.

Her aunt had always tyrannised her in an effort to curb her wilfulness, but to try and force her into a marriage with a man—who must seem as old as Methuselah to a young girl—was sheer folly on her aunt's part. Who could blame Katherine for running away?

Blake's expression softened, taking Katherine by surprise when he spoke more gently. 'I know you didn't. This is not going to be an easy time for either of us. Now—do as I ask and go to your room. I am aware of the antagonism that exists between you and your aunt and I shall try and do my best to smooth the way for you. But I cannot do that if you see her just now.'

Oddly touched by the change in his voice and the look in his eyes, Katherine nodded and without a word turned from him. Blake watched until she had disappeared up the stairs before going in search of his stepmother. Not a woman he was particularly fond of, but she had been his father's wife and, as such, he had always treated her with the respect her position warranted. Fortunately, because of his naval career, he'd had little to do with her over the years.

CHAPTER THREE

AN AIR of oppression hung over Ludgrove Hall.
Servants moved with stealth about the house, afraid
of raising their voices above a whisper. Henry was
brought home from Oxford at the same time that
Amelia and her husband arrived from London,
having accompanied Lord Russell's body back to
Ludgrove.

Confined to her room and still not having spoken
to her aunt, who Matilda said was bearing up well
after the shock her husband's death had caused her,
Katherine was glad to see Amelia, whose features
were so like Blake's but without his serious countenance. Amelia had a warm and open manner and she
and Katherine had always been close. Although
deeply saddened by her father's death Amelia was
more in control of her emotions than Matilda, who
was inconsolable and in the habit of bursting into
uncontrollable sobbing whenever he was mentioned.

Lord Russell had been much loved and respected
by most people in Appleby. As the solemn cortège
moved slowly from Ludgrove Hall to the village
church where he was to be interred with his ances-
tors, the road was lined with all the estate workers
tied to Ludgrove Hall, the great house—the bailiffs

48

and tenant farmers, whose rents supplied most of the Russells' wealth, the herdsmen, the shepherds, the keepers and foresters, who maintained the deer park, the thatchers, the carpenters and masons, who built or maintained all the buildings on the Russell estate, all there to pay their last respects. Bowing their bare heads, hats clapped to their chests, silent as they watched, wondering about the changes his passing would make to their own lives now his son had taken over.

But many suspected already that there were dark days ahead, that whatever changes the new Lord Russell made to his estate would be like a drop in the ocean compared to what might happen in the country as a whole. The general atmosphere in England was one of restlessness and uncertainty, brought about by a trade depression, unemployment and the plague. After a vain attempt in sixteen thirty-nine to suppress the rising of his Scottish subjects, the King had been compelled, after eleven years, to call another Parliament to Westminster asking for financial aid, and now the whole country was united in its grievances over forced loans and taxes which many refused to pay. It was being whispered that Civil War was probable and pamphleteers had never been so busy, but in the main people prayed that peace might somehow prevail.

It was several days later that Amelia and Katherine, accompanied by Thomas, one of the grooms, rode down the busy main street that ran through the centre of Appleby, which was flanked on either side by small thatched cottages. They were just passing the village inn, The Black Boar, when Katherine's horse chose that moment to shed one of its shoes. Fortunately the day was unseasonably warm, so they sat and waited at one of the tables outside the inn whilst Thomas took the horse off to the blacksmith's across the street. Honoured to have such important guests, the innkeeper brought them some lemonade to drink while they waited.

As they chatted Katherine's eyes went past Amelia to where a young man was sitting outside the inn some distance away, abstractedly staring down at a leatherbound book in his lap. She noticed how the sun shone on his head, bowed slightly as he read, his fair, silken tresses tied neatly back with a ribbon in the nape of his neck. He was of slender build and Katherine imagined he would be quite tall when standing.

He looked to be in his mid-twenties, an intelligent, thinking sort of gentleman, out of place here at the inn among rural folk. He would be better suited to one of the towns of learning, she thought, staring at him with frank curiosity, but then her attention was claimed by Amelia.

'It seems that your escapade with Lord Forbes has created a fine bit of gossip for the folk in Appleby, Katherine,' she said, indicating a couple of gossiping women across the street who kept throwing meaningful, conspiratorial glances their way.

'It appears so,' she sighed. 'I do find it all so very tiresome. I was hoping that with all the attention paid to your father's passing, interest in my own indiscretion would be brief.'

'It will pass when something else occurs to give them something to gossip about. No one will think the less of you. Although, I must say that it seems to be taking your aunt some time to get over it. I doubt she'll recover in a hurry from your running off with Lord Forbes.'

'But I didn't run off with him, Amelia,' said Katherine emphatically. 'You know I wouldn't do that. I merely asked him to take me with him to London. Nothing happened. Lord Forbes tried to compromise me so that I would have had little choice but to marry him. Blake, thank goodness, intervened.'

'Matilda told me you were running away to avoid marriage to Sir George Carrington. Is this true?'

'Yes. I was going to come to you, Amelia. I would rather die than wed Sir George. Marriage to Lord Forbes would be preferable to that.'

Amelia laughed. 'I quite see what you mean, Katherine—although if I were you I would beware of such men. Lord Forbes has quite a wicked reputation at Court. His father led the most lavish, dissolute life imaginable; should his son acquire the means then he would be no better. However, much good it would have done you to come to me for, regardless of what I had to say about you remaining in London—where I would have had such fun showing you around—Blake would have been furious and ordered you to return to Ludgrove Hall at once.'

Katherine's eyes clouded at the mention of Blake. 'Whatever I do seems to meet with his displeasure. All I ever do is provoke his anger. In his eyes I have very few virtues.'

'Oh, come now, Katherine,' said Amelia quickly. 'I'm sure he doesn't mean to be angry with you. You have to understand him—and your own resentful attitude whenever he is present is apparent to him.'

Katherine frowned crossly from across the table. 'Why, Amelia—I'm sure I don't know what you mean.'

Amelia loved Katherine as she would her natural sister and was not afraid to speak her mind. 'Yes, you do. You know, Katherine, Father's death is going to make a profound difference to Blake's life. It isn't going to be easy for him having to adjust to life on dry land. He loved the sea—his ship and his crew. It was his life.

'There hasn't been much room for family matters in his life for quite some time. Perhaps if Henry were older and could shoulder some of the responsibilities of the estate, then it might relieve some of the pressure but, as it is, Henry must complete his studies. Although I imagine that now Blake is home for good his marriage to Margaret will go ahead.

Having someone by his side should alleviate some of the pressure.'

Katherine lowered her eyes so that Amelia would not see the pain her words had caused her, saying a silent prayer of apology for the fierce joy she would be sure to feel if his marriage did not take place.

'Unlike Father,' Amelia continued, 'Blake was born with a spirit of adventure and independence. Oh,' she laughed, 'and with an insufferable arrogance which everyone is aware of. But I do not believe you have need to fear him. Beneath his many moods I believe he is extremely fond of you.'

Feeling that Amelia was being kind to spare her feelings, Katherine sighed wistfully. 'I know and I shall always be grateful for the kindness he showed me when I first came to Ludgrove. But of late he has been so disagreeable. I don't believe he sees me half of the time.'

'Come now, Katherine, you misjudge him. My dear brother hasn't seen you for almost two years— I am sure the change in you has come as something of a shock to him. Haven't you looked in the mirror recently? You, my dear, have become a very beautiful young woman. No man in his right mind, unless he is short-sighted, could fail to notice you. In London you would be all the rage. If you come some time, it will give me great pleasure to take you under my wing and have you presented at Court.'

'I would like that,' smiled Katherine, delighted at the prospect. 'But I doubt Aunt Harriet or your

brother would allow it. How I wish I had some say
in my life. Suddenly your brother thinks he is my
keeper.'

'Well, in a way he is—while ever you live under
his roof, that is. But don't worry. For the short time
I remain at Ludgrove I shall try and keep him out of
your way as much as possible.'

'There is something much more important that
you can do for me,' Katherine said seriously. 'When
you do return to London the day after tomorrow,
will you try and persuade him to let me go with
you?'

Amelia did not hesitate in her reply. 'I will try,'
she said, draining her tankard. 'But you know how
stubborn he can be and anyway—your aunt may still
insist on you marrying Sir George.'

Katherine looked at her steadily. 'I won't marry
him, Amelia, not ever. And with any luck he won't
want to marry a woman whose reputation has been
sullied.'

'Mmm,' murmured Amelia, not convinced, for she
was aware of the power money had over impover-
ished gentlemen. 'He may be prepared to overlook
that. After all, your dowry is quite considerable.' She
rose suddenly. 'Come. See—Thomas is waving to us.
He is ready to leave. We don't want to give your
aunt cause to reproach us. She'll never believe your
horse lost a shoe.'

Conscious of the young gentleman's continued
regard, Katherine turned her head as she was about

to follow Amelia. She met his direct gaze, which did not falter. Though some distance away, she could see that his eyes were as blue as her own, with faint laughter lines at the corners. Unselfconsciously, she studied him. His look was thoughtful and inquisitive—his eyes did not light up with flattery or admiration as was often the case when men looked at her. He smiled, his teeth white and even, and then he rose, bowing his head courteously in her direction before disappearing inside the inn. Katherine climbed onto her horse, still thinking of him. It had been a casual encounter which she found disquieting and puzzling, one which was temporarily forgotten on reaching Ludgrove Hall.

When they rode into the stable yard Blake strode across the cobbles to meet them, his lean sunburned face breaking into a warm smile, his eyes lighting up with pleasure when they came to rest on his beloved sister. Reaching up, he assisted her to dismount.

'You look pleased with yourself,' he said. 'You've had an enjoyable ride, I take it?'

'Extremely,' Amelia replied, 'apart from Katherine's mare losing a shoe. Fortunately it happened close to the blacksmith's so Thomas was able to have it reshod while we took refreshment at The Black Boar. I was just telling Katherine about life at Court.'

'Now that should be interesting,' laughed Blake lightly, moving towards where Katherine still sat on her horse. Reaching up, he placed his hands on her waist, lifted her down and set her gently on her feet. He did not let her go immediately; the firm clasp of his hands remained on her trim waist as he looked deep into her eyes. 'And what of you, Mistress Blair? Is that what you would like? To be presented at the Court of King Charles?'

His warm strong grip disturbed Katherine, stirring up dark, hidden pleasures deep within her, but she managed to school her features to express nothing but polite interest to his question.

'Why—I would deem it an honour—as anyone would. It would certainly be interesting and exciting,' she answered. But, she asked herself as he continued to hold her gaze, was it what she wanted if going to London meant being away from him? If remaining at Ludgrove Hall meant seeing him married to Lady Margaret—which would be too painful for her to bear—and the threat of marriage to Sir George, or some other as disagreeable to her, remained, then yes, she would rather be in London.

'I doubt there is much excitement at this time,' he said releasing her, trying not to think of how fetching she looked in her dark blue habit, the ribbons of her hair and hat of the same colour, emphasising the whiteness of her skin and the deep rich colour of her golden hair.

'Oh, and why do you say that, pray?' asked Amelia, turning away, smiling slowly to herself, having observed the way Blake had looked at

Katherine, how his hands had lingered too long on her waist after lifting her from her horse. It seemed her brother was not as immune to her charms as Katherine thought. But what of Lady Margaret? wondered Amelia. Was he beginning to forget how lovely and charming she was after such a long period of absence?

Together the three of them walked across the cobbles towards the house as the grooms led the horses away.

'The recent riots in London should speak for themselves,' Blake continued, referring to the previous December when there had been an uprising of the apprentices of the city.

The political and economic crisis in England had caused chronic unemployment, providing a reservoir of idle youths and men. They had descended with arms on Parliament, demanding that bishops be excluded from government and the church. The violence of the mob had been so extreme that the King, afraid for the safety of his own household, had been forced to form a corps of guards as protection.

'Did you tell Mistress Blair how the Court of King Charles revolves mainly about the Queen and her frivolous friends?'

'And what is wrong with that, pray?' said Amelia with fervour. 'It is hardly the place of sinful pleasure as it was in his father's time—in fact, the Court of King Charles is the most formal in the whole of Europe. Were it not for the Queen's fondness for dancing and penchant for the theatre, then it would be an exceedingly dull place indeed.'

'It is not the Queen's licensed gaiety I object to but her Catholic cohorts—who will not be satisfied until England comes once again under the rule of Rome. I've had little time to give to religious matters these past months but I have always been of the opinion that the King, under the influence of his strongly Catholic Queen, is an inadmissable danger to Protestant England. Even your husband, my dear sister, has expressed his concern that you spend too much time in the company of her papal retinue— that you have even visited her chapel at Somerset House.'

'And so I have. Out of curiosity, nothing more— and one cannot fail to be impressed by its beauty. I assure you, Blake, that I have no more intention of becoming a convert to Catholicism than I have to Presbyterianism, if that is what you are afraid of.'

'Heaven forbid that should be the case,' Blake laughed, a deep rich sound. Katherine, listening to the light banter between brother and sister, was glad to see he had shaken off some of the gloom which had been present since his father's death.

'And by all accounts,' he went on, glancing sideways wickedly at his sister, 'you are not averse to the attentions of the licentious young gallants who frequent the Court.'

'Ha!' she exclaimed good-humouredly. 'And I remember a time—not so very long ago, either—

when you could be named as one of them. Methinks you have been at sea too long, Blake, and the sun has addled your memory. Recollect the time when you were one of those wild young courtiers seeking additional pleasures away from the good taste and manners of the Court—be it at the gaming tables of Piccadilly, the race track of Hyde Park or the pleasure gardens south of the river. The taverns of Westminster and the Strand held no secrets from you, either.'

Blake laughed. 'You know me too well, Amelia.'

'Too well, brother.' She paused, looking from her brother to Katherine, suddenly curious. 'And what nonsense is this, Blake—that you should address Katherine as Mistress Blair? I remember a time when you used to call her Katherine—and you, Katherine, addressing Blake as "My lord", making him sound so grand? It is quite ridiculous. Why, since you came to live at Ludgrove Hall you have been more like a sister to us all.'

Katherine's eyes met Blake's, which shone with derisive humour. She tossed her head, instantly on the defensive.

'It was your brother who introduced the formality between us when he took to addressing me as Mistress Blair.' But, yes, she did remember a time when he used to address her as Katherine, a time wich would remain one of her most treasured memories and which now seemed to belong to another life. She looked at him, waiting for him to respond to Amelia's question. A smile moved across his lean brown face.

'Well, Blake?' prompted Amelia. 'What have you to say?'

He gave Katherine a cool, sardonic look. 'It may have escaped your notice, Amelia, but Mistress Blair is no longer the girl she was when she first came to live at Ludgrove Hall. And nor is she my sister to be treated and spoken to as I would you or Matilda. She is our stepmother's niece and no blood relative.'

Secretly he thanked the Lord that she was not his sister—by the way she had begun to appeal to his senses, the desire he felt whenever he looked at her would be quite incestuous. She was beginning to trouble him greatly. It would be a relief when she had found a husband and was no longer within his sight. 'I trust it suits you that I continue to call you Mistress Blair? That it gives no offence?'

There was mockery in his voice and a challenge in his dark eyes which caused hot angry words to bubble to Katherine's lips which, with difficulty, she checked, although she seethed inwardly, angry that they should talk of her as if she were not present.

'No, my lord,' she replied haughtily, longing to slap the arrogant smile from his lips with her riding whip. 'It suits me well enough.'

'I am relieved to hear it. Oh, and I almost forgot to tell you,' he said, his eyes holding hers, very much aware of the effect of what he had to say would have on her, 'your aunt was asking for you. She wishes to see you on your return from your ride.'

Katherine paled. 'I will go right away. Pray—excuse me.' She turned and, with a dignified step, hurried on ahead of them. This was what she had dreaded ever since Blake had brought her back to Ludgrove Hall in disgrace. If it had not been for Lord Russell's death, no doubt she would have been summoned sooner.

Linking her arm through Blake's, Amelia watched her go before giving him a reproachful look. 'Blake—how could you? That was downright wicked.'

He sighed. 'Wicked? Perhaps.' He spoke absently, his eyes following Katherine thoughtfully as she went on ahead of them. 'I am merely trying to preserve my own sanity.'

Katherine stood facing her aunt, consumed with dread. It was the first time they had spoken since the day she had told her she was to marry Sir George Carrington, although she had been aware of her deep displeasure since then. She stood waiting for her to speak—or erupt. The eyes that bore into hers were as cold as ice. Unable to stand the silence or her aunt's scrutiny a moment longer Katherine spoke quietly.

'You wish to see me, Aunt?'

'No—but I thought it was time I did,' Harriet said coldly. 'The grief I suffer over the death of my

husband is overshadowed by the shame you have
brought on us all. Your defiance and the gossip
directed against the whole family, brought about by
your scandalous behaviour, the pointing fingers and
malicious whisperings, are all too much. When I
learned what you had done—running off with Lord
Forbes, Sir George's guest of all people—I found it
hard to believe—even of you, Katherine.'

'I am deeply sorry to have caused you so much
trouble but I could not marry Sir George. Not out of
duty or even gratitude to you, Aunt, for all you have
done for me. But I was not running off with Lord
Forbes. He—he was taking me to Amelia.'

'So I understand from Blake. Although there is
little difference to my mind. You left this house
without a chaperon or a word to anyone. If you had
not been seen climbing into Sir George's carriage
then no one would have known what had become of
you and feared the worst. I understand that Lord
Forbes took advantage of the situation and tried to
compromise you. Well,' she said, taking a deep angry
breath, 'it would serve you right if I insisted on you
marrying him instead of Sir George.'

'I have not changed my mind,' said Katherine
steadily. 'I still refuse to wed Sir George.'

'And what makes you think he still wants you?
Your reputation is in ruins. Even if you changed
your mind and agreed to marry him it would be
futile, for in the light of what has happened he has

withdrawn his proposal—and I have to say that I cannot blame him.'

At the absolute relief that flooded Katherine's eyes her aunt's anger increased.

'So, that pleases you, does it?' she hissed through gritted teeth, breathing deeply in an effort to control her anger. 'I had hoped you might regret the folly of your wildness but it seems that is not so. I had hoped to find more submission in you—obedience, even, but I see it is not in your nature.'

'I cannot change my nature, Aunt,' whispered Katherine, feeling the tension between them increasing.

Enraged by what she considered to be Katherine's insolence, Harriet became even more incensed. 'You ungrateful girl,' she fumed. 'Why—you are just like your mother after all. Her ingratitude to your father was unforgivable, also.'

Katherine looked at her, her eyes widening in puzzlement. 'What has my mother to do with any of this? And why should she have felt the need to be grateful to my father?'

'He married her, didn't he?' replied her aunt with seething contempt. 'It is high time you knew what kind of woman she was.' Anger had made the blood rush to her face. She gave a shrill laugh that sounded ugly and brought a deadly glitter to her eyes. She looked so frighteningly angry that Katherine almost turned and fled the room.

Katherine had always been aware of the hatred

her aunt felt for her mother, whose name was never mentioned between them. The reason for this hatred had always remained a secret to her but she felt it must be something deep and profound. Suspecting that her aunt was about to enlighten her as to her mother's character she turned away, unwilling to hear anything to discredit her.

'Pray excuse me, but I will not stay and listen to anything you might say that is disparaging about my mother.'

'Oh, yes, miss, you will listen. For too long have I allowed you to live in ignorance. I can see only one reason for your disgraceful behaviour—which I am certain is caused by the bad blood inherited from your mother.'

Katherine turned, facing her aunt with defiance in every line of her body. 'My mother died giving birth to me. Even though I did not know her, I shall cherish her memory forever. Do not tarnish that, Aunt, for I will never forgive you.'

'So your father would have had you believe—that she died giving birth to you in an attempt to hide the filthy truth: your mother was a whore. She did not care for your father. The man she loved—whose bed she had wallowed in and whose child she had conceived when she wed your father—was married to another.'

Katherine was filled with an overriding horror at what she was hearing. She felt as though she were encased in ice as she listened to her aunt's ravings.

The whole world seemed to be rocking about her. And then a thought, a thought so monstrous occurred to her that she was almost too afraid to ask the question that sprung to her lips.

'Are—are you telling me that—that my father was not—?'

'Oh, never fear—he was your father. You came later. The child she was carrying—that she paraded so insolently about his house—was her lover's child. Your half-brother.'

No, screamed a voice inside Katherine's head as she stared at her aunt in bewilderment, trying to comprehend what she was saying. 'Brother? I have a brother?'

'Aye, and dead or alive after these many years I care not one way or another. Your mother was unable to marry the boy's father—who was also your own father's close friend. Like a fool your father worshipped her. She could do no wrong in his eyes. He believed her firstborn to be his own son. After you were born, things began to go wrong between them. It was mainly to do with her faith. She was a Catholic, you see, and he despised Catholicism. When he insisted that you and your brother should be brought up in the Protestant faith the truth came out and she told him he had fathered a bastard. Only then did he do what he should have done from the start. He turned her and her child out.'

Katherine stared at her, sick with horror at what she had been told. Feeling a lightness inside her

head she swayed slightly, gripping the back of a chair
firmly, praying she would not faint. After a moment
she regained control of herself, breathing deeply.

'What happened to my mother? Where did she
go?'

'That I do not know.'

'And my brother?'

'I do not know that, either.'

'What was his name?' she asked, wanting and yet
dreading to know all there was to know about her
unknown brother.

'I don't remember. Edward—or something like it.'

Katherine looked at her aunt coldly. 'You could
have spared me this and gone on with the deception.
Why tell me now?'

'Because I have reached the limits of my endur-
ance where you are concerned,' she hissed. 'I believe
it is time you knew what sort of woman your mother
was.'

Wanting to remain faithful to her mother's
memory, Katherine had every intention of giving her
the benefit of the doubt. 'I doubt it is as sordid as
you would have me believe, Aunt. Is there nothing
more you can tell me?'

'Why? So that you can go looking for them—
bringing further shame on us all? It is best that you
think of them as dead.'

'Does anyone else know of this? Does—does
Blake know?'

'No—and it will stay that way. Is it not enough

that he has to house an obstinate and unruly girl under his roof without him knowing your mother was a slut?'

Katherine's cheeks burned with indignation and heated words rose to her lips in defence of her mother, regardless of what she had just been told, but her aunt silenced her before she could utter a word.

'I shall continue to do my duty towards you as your guardian, which is what your father requested of me, and see that a husband is found for you as soon as possible—for the sooner you are no longer in my care and I do not have to deal with your disobedience, the better it will be for us all.'

How Katherine got back to her room she could not remember, for she could think of nothing other than the fact that her mother might still be alive and somewhere she had a brother. She tried telling herself that none of what her aunt had told her was true, but then she realised that it must be, that it was the reason why her father had told her almost nothing at all of her mother. She had always supposed that this was because he had loved her so much that it pained him to speak of her. But now she knew it went much deeper than that. Her aunt had told her that he had worshipped her mother. Had he stopped loving her when he had learned the truth and banished her and her son from his life forever? And what of her mother? Where had she gone? Had she missed the child she had left behind? These were questions her mother alone could answer.

No matter what her aunt had said, she could not think of her or her brother as dead. How could she find them? The house in Rochester had been sold on the death of her father. The questions which tormented her must all remain unanswered for now, but never had Katherine felt so lost, helpless and alone and, she thought bitterly, never had she wanted to leave Ludgrove Hall as much as she did just then, even if it meant leaving Blake.

CHAPTER FOUR

IN DESPERATION the following day Katherine went in search of Blake, hoping she could persuade him to have a word with her aunt on her behalf so that she might leave with Amelia. After all if, as her aunt had said, he considered her to be an obstinate and unruly girl, then maybe he would be happy to be rid of her. But if she had thought this, then she was mistaken.

Katherine faced him in his study. On hearing her reason for seeking him out, his expression became hard.

'Amelia has mentioned the matter to me but I prefer you to remain here for the time being.'

Katherine stared at him with understandable dismay. 'But why?' she asked. 'I cannot understand why you are so set against my going with Amelia. Since I seem to have such a disruptive influence I cannot see why you are so insistent that I remain.'

'And I cannot for the life of me see where you have got the notion that I consider you a disruptive influence. You have had one fall from grace; I am merely trying to ensure there will not be a second. That is all. I hope I have never given you reason to believe that I have an aversion to your living in this house—quite the contrary, in fact. Ludgrove Hall is as much your home as it is Matilda's or Henry's for as long as you choose to make it so.'

'Or until my aunt orders me to marry.' Katherine's expression became one of desperation as she moved towards him. 'Please,' she implored, 'I would so like to leave with Amelia.'

Blake looked at her curiously, wondering what had happened to make her so desperate to leave Ludgrove Hall. She wouldn't normally appeal to him in this manner.

'May I ask what transpired between you and your aunt yesterday to bring about this apparent urgency to leave?'

Katherine's expression changed quickly, her face becoming like a closed book. 'Why—nothing. Nothing at all. It is no secret that my aunt and I have never been able to see eye to eye. And, anyway, I am not obliged to discuss the matter with you.'

Blake frowned, curious as to what lay behind her lowered lids. He realised just how much she had changed in the two years since he had last seen her. There was no sign of the buoyant, unruly adolescent girl. Now there was about her a strange new quality he had not known she possessed. She was poised, with a gentleness and a heartwarming charm; at that moment he was trying hard not to let his mind dwell on how lovely she looked lest it weakened his resolve for, however hard she pleaded with him he would not let her go with Amelia. Not with the villainous Lord Forbes at liberty in London.

'No,' he answered coldly. 'You forget how well I know my sister, for however much I adore her, I know she will take every opportunity of dangling you under the nose of every eligible male at Court. Given the circumstances I have no intention of allowing you to make yourself ridiculous. Also, I am well aware that Lord Forbes will be at Court. I think we ought to allow time for the attention your misdemeanour has attracted to settle down before you flaunt yourself abroad.'

Katherine stared at him with growing anger. 'And who is to say Lord Forbes will notice me among all the beautiful ladies who grace the Court?' she fumed. 'The chances are he has forgotten all about me.'

'You underestimate your charms, Mistress Blair,' Blake said dryly. 'Of course he will notice you. He is hardly likely to forget the circumstances of your last meeting.'

'And what if I take it upon myself to leave?' said Katherine in defiance.

A gleam of anger showed in Blake's eyes. His features hardened as he wondered how he could have been foolish enough to believe she had changed. She was still the same wilful girl he remembered of old.

When he spoke, his tone was merciless and cutting. 'I do not advise it, for then you would find you had not only your aunt's displeasure to contend with but my own. So—let that be an end to the matter. The subject is no longer open to discussion. You are not going to London and that is final. I shall lock you in your chamber if need be.'

'As you did that night at the inn?' she scorned.

'If you like—and with a guard outside if necessary. I think you've caused enough mischief for the time being. Heaven only knows what devilment you would get up to under my sister's guidance at Court. I'd be failing in my duty if I let you go, and I am certain your aunt would agree with me.'

Katherine set her chin mutinously and they glared at each other like two combatants. 'You, my lord, are a tyrant and you do your sister an injustice. You also take your *duty* towards myself too far. You play the role of an aggressive brother or father whose family honour has been besmirched by my indiscretion. You said yourself that I am nothing to you— that I am no blood relation—so stop behaving as my guardian.'

Blake moved towards her, his eyes, narrowing dangerously, glittering like two black coals. Katherine should have known better than to provoke him to further anger but her own anger was such that she was unable to stop.

'No, Mistress Blair, not your guardian—merely the master of this house, and while you live under my roof you will conduct yourself in a fit and proper manner.'

'Why, what is it?' Katherine scoffed, caring not that she goaded him further, for to her mind his refusal to let her go to London with Amelia had turned him into a monster puffed up with ruthless pride. 'Are you afraid that I might begin to enjoy myself—to feel pleasure at being admired? That I might be desired by the gentlemen of the Court? If so, what is so ridiculous about that, pray? Perhaps you have been at sea so long that you have forgotten the meaning of the word.'

Blake's look became one of thunder. Instinctively, Katherine turned from him, intending to leave the room, but taking a step towards her, with a quick movement he reached out and swung her round to face him, gripped her shoulders and drew her towards him with a force which made her cry out in surprise. She stared up at him. He was breathing heavily, his eyes burning down into hers, his expression hard, and she was suddenly afraid of the violent force her disobedience had unleashed in him. She had dared to taunt him and that alone was enough reason for him to teach her that he was not a man to be made a mockery of.

'So, you believe I do not know the meaning of the word desire,' he said with sarcasm, his face close to hers, causing her to tremble at the naked passion which shone from the depths of his eyes. 'Let me tell you that it is an emotion I am well acquainted with, one which I can prove very simply.'

Suddenly he drew her into his arms and, before

Katherine could resist or utter one word of protest, his lips were on hers, hard and demanding. He began to kiss her ardently. Taken utterly by surprise, she struggled against him, but Blake was a man in full possession of his strength and she didn't stand a chance. She felt herself weakening and slowly began to melt within his arms, the pressure of his embrace not nearly as disturbing as the pleasure his kiss aroused. His lips left hers and travelled slowly down her neck, burying themselves in the soft curve of her throat before finding her lips once more. But he released her as suddenly as he had caught her to him.

Shaken to the core by what had happened, they looked silently at each other. This new turn of events was more than either of them had expected for, no matter how attracted he was by her, Blake had no intention of becoming involved with her in any way. How could he, when he was betrothed to another? He stared at Katherine's lovely face, framed by her golden hair flowing down her back. He noticed how her young breasts strained beneath the bodice of her gown, how her moist lips trembled as she tilted her head slightly to look at him. How could he have let such a thing happen? He cursed himself for his weakness and stupidity, having to turn away to escape the soft bewitchment in her wonderful, imploring eyes.

'My apologies, Mistress Blair,' he said curtly, managing to regain most of his composure. 'I forgot my manners. I have done you a wrong and Margaret, my betrothed, an even greater wrong. I assure you it will not happen again.'

Her shoulders tender from the grip of his hands, Katherine stared with confusion at the closed door for a long time after he had gone, for his kiss had kindled a spark of hope in her heart—for now, her cup of happiness was brimming over.

Not normally given to displays of emotion, Blake had taken her in his arms with a passion sharpened by anger, forgetting everything—even the fair Lady Margaret. He had tried to throw a cloak over what had passed between them, apologising, telling her it would not happen again, and her instinct told her that already he must be tortured with self-castigation as he angrily reproached himself for his weakness of having given way to his feelings. But sooner or later they would have to meet. How would he react to her then? she wondered, experiencing a heady exultation, a sweet joy, knowing that she had the power to make him want her after all. But deep down inside her she knew that the love she carried for him in her heart was still an impossible dream.

The following day Henry returned to Oxford and Amelia and her husband left for London without Katherine, whose mind was filled with confusion over what had transpired the previous day. It had been dominated by two events: the first, the shattering discovery that she had a half-brother and that her mother might still be alive; the second, Blake's kiss.

When the euphoria of his embrace had worn off, it was like waking from a dream, one that Katherine had been living on, feeding on, for a long time, and her face had become hot with shame when she had begun to see her folly in a true light. The kiss had changed everything—things would never be the same between her and Blake again. She had felt that she had lost a happiness which had never been hers in the first place, and in that bitterest moment of all she had looked clearly at her situation as it was.

Blake was betrothed to Lady Margaret Tawney, committed to her. Margaret was the one who would live with him, share his thoughts, sleep in his arms at night, bear his children, not her. Margaret trusted him, loved him, probably as much as she did herself, and for this reason she must abandon any hope that he would turn from Margaret to her.

Katherine had remembered the one time she had met Lady Margaret, when she had come to Ludgrove Hall two years ago with her brother to see Blake, before there had been any romantic attachment between them; she had liked her, warmed to her, and she would not wish to hurt her in any way.

Although Blake had been against her going to London with Amelia, she could see that now it would be unwise for her to remain at Ludgrove Hall close to him. Her aunt was keen for her to marry— maybe that was the answer. But she could not marry someone she did not love and it would be a long time, if ever, before she would be able to rid her mind of Blake's image, or her heart of the love she carried, and it was going to make all the difference to her feelings for anyone else.

Over the following days that ran into weeks, Katherine never saw Blake alone. She understood how busy he was as he familiarised himself with the running of the estate, pouring over ledgers with his bailiff, tending to the needs of the tenant farmers, returning to the house with his thick hair tied back, his handsome features thoughtful as he contemplated some new problem that had presented itself.

On the occasions when they had met at meal times, when he had addressed her his voice had always been cold and terse. She might just as well have been transparent for he had seemed to look right through her. He had distanced himself from her completely, evading her about the house, and his determination to ignore her presence had hurt and had offended her deeply, reawakening all her old doubts and fears that he had cared nothing for her after all.

Katherine became quiet and withdrawn as she began to consider how she might discover further information about what had become of her mother and brother all those years ago. Her aunt would tell her no more than she already had, saying that what had been was dead and buried. Why couldn't she leave it that way? But, no, God help her, she could not. Curiosity and the need to know drove her on.

Had she been free to do so, she would have made for Rochester at once to see if there was anyone who remembered her mother, but fear of being caught by Blake and brought back to Ludgrove Hall, bringing further disgrace upon herself and the family, made her dismiss the idea. Besides, she had no wish to divulge to Blake what her aunt had told her, preferring to keep it to herself. Her mother had been a Catholic. Knowing of Blake's aversion to anyone of that faith, and with the present resurgence of hate and persecutions throughout the country directed against them, then the things about her mother's past could be dangerous to her own present safety.

She would have to find some other way of finding out what had become of them. But how else could she go about it? There was no way that she could see. If still alive, they could be anywhere. With reluctance Katherine had to admit that she could do nothing at this time. But she would not let it lie and was fiercely determined to pursue the matter when she was no longer her aunt's charge.

Life at Ludgrove Hall went on as usual until one day, at dinner—which was eaten at midday—her aunt announced without prior warning that Blake was to leave for London. Katherine's heart contracted with pain and Matilda immediately dropped her napkin onto her plate, looking across the table at her beloved brother with dismay.

'Blake—no. Why—you've only recently arrived back home. After all those years you were absent I—I thought—I hoped you were back to stay. Will you be away for long?'

'I don't know as yet. What with the government all in pieces and our ships lying idle in the dock, trade is so depressed that I must go and see what can be done. The tonnage and poundage which has been levied by the King, without the consent of Parliament, is causing much discontent among the merchants, and the increased taxation on imported tobacco has affected the profits of the Western Trading Company considerably.'

It was these very taxes which had forced Blake's father to spend much of his time in London, overseeing the running of the company. Blake was certain that the stress brought about by this had proved too much for his Father and had resulted in his fatal seizure.

'Also,' he went on, 'the Earl of Strafford's trial has provoked riots, with armed mobs roaming the streets—many of them out-of-work mariners and dockers. I could be gone for quite gome time.'

Blake's eyes came to rest on Katherine where she sat directly across from him, the table between them laden with a gargantuan side of roast mutton and other dishes. She sat with her back ramrod straight, her golden hair forming a glistening bright halo in

the sunlight streaming through the window behind
her. Her eyes were fixed steadily on his.

Blake had observed a change in her of late. Her
smile was no longer spontaneous and, when she was
with Matilda, he noticed that her laugh, once unself-
conscious, sounded artificial. He was disturbed by
this change in her, suspecting she was angry because
she had not been allowed to go with Amelia to
London.

Or could it be that, after what had passed between
them, she felt shy and awkward in his presence? But
then he bethought himself and frowned. Awkward?
Possibly. But shy? Never. She still had a look of
defiance, he thought, and impatience as she carefully
kept her temperament in check. How would she take
what he had to say to her?

'Your aunt and I are in agreement that you will
accompany me to London, Mistress Blair.'

'Seeing that no gentleman of worth in the district
seems to want anything to do with you,' said her
aunt scathingly, 'we think it best that you go to
London after all. Your chances of acquiring a husband will be increased somewhat at Court. The
scandal you created should have subsided by now.
Amelia has agreed for you to stay with her, and
Blake will be there to see to it that you behave in a
proper and ladylike manner.'

Katherine's hands were trembling as they gripped
the arms of her chair. She wanted to shout that she
did not want a husband. For so long she had res-

olutely pushed any idea of going to London from her mind. Now, all of a sudden, quite unexpectedly, here was her aunt telling her that she was to go and that she was to go with Blake.

New life began to flow through her veins but nothing of what she was feeling showed on her face, which took on a calm serenity that was shattered a moment later by Blake's next words, forcing her mind back to painful reality.

'The Earl of Rockley will also be in London with Margaret who is eager to set the date for our wedding. However, that should not interfere with what is planned for you.' He lazily elevated one brow. 'Come, Mistress Blair. What have you to say? Is this not what you wanted?'

Katherine stopped her hands from trembling by placing them in her lap, her eyes as blue as the temperate speedwell. She continued to look at him steadily, giving no indication of her thoughts, of how much seeing him with Lady Margaret Tawney would pain her.

'Yes, I shall be glad to go, and I am sure Lady Margaret must be impatient to see you after so long an absence.'

Blake frowned. How small her voice sounded, he thought, pure and childlike, and this somehow pierced his armour. The sensations she had aroused in him the day that he had kissed her surged through him anew. He was perplexed by the strong emotions he had felt as her lips had opened under his, yielding a sweetness which had made him want to drink his fill.

He was taking her to London in the hope of finding her a husband, but, strangely, the thought of her with another man—in his arms, kissing him, lying with him—disgusted him. He was confused and this angered him. He told himself that only when she was wed and he was married to Margaret would he be purged of these feelings.

'When are you to leave?' asked Matilda, looking as if she would cry in a moment, so distressed was she at the thought of losing Katherine. What on earth would she do without her?

'A few days—no more,' Blake replied.

'Can I not go with Katherine?' she asked, looking across at her brother beseechingly.

'No, Matilda,' said her mother sharply, for she had high hopes of the young gentlemen in the district taking an interest in her once Katherine was out of the way. 'You will stay here.'

Matilda turned quickly to her mother, an anxious look on her face. 'But if, as Blake says, there are armed mobs roaming the streets, surely it is unwise that Katherine should be subjected to such danger?'

'It is true there is serious unrest in London,' said Blake calmly, not wishing to alarm them further, but his stepmother fixed him with a hard questioning look. He knew she would not be deceived into believing all was well with the nation.

'Just how serious is it, Blake?' she asked.

''Tis serious enough. As well you know, there is deep resentment over the new prayer book the King has imposed on his subjects in England, and Scotland where it has stirred up a hornets' nest. The Scots are a fiercely independent people and are up in arms, resenting anything imposed on them from England. They have drawn up a National Covenant in defence of their Kirk. The King has been forced to summon Parliament to ask for subsidies to subdue them, but unless he satisfies their demands with regards to their religion then he must provide the means to fight them. I believe England is drifting towards crsis.'

'Civil war?' asked Harriet bluntly.

Blake nodded slowly, his expression grave. 'It could come to that, although his soldiers do not want a war with Scotland, for if it is to be about a matter of religion, then they would rather direct their discontent against the Catholics within their midst, than against the covenanting Scots. The King's actions have become the subject of much criticism, some of it related to the fact that he does little to quell the growth of Popery in England which is poisoning the waters of Protestantism.

'Feelings are running high, with people clamouring for the abolition of episcopacy and the head of Strafford. And more is to follow, for we must not forget that William Laud, the Archbishop of Canterbury, languishes in the Tower awaiting trial.

Like Strafford, he too worked in the King's best interests before being accused of high treason.

'I have told you that riots are commonplace on the streets, resulting in damage to people and property. Our own offices of business close to the Royal Exchange have suffered some considerable damage which I must repair.'

'The Earl of Strafford,' whispered Matilda with something like dread, for many of the tales she had heard about him had made him into something of a bogey man. 'He's the one they call "Black Tom Tyrant", isn't he? Will he be executed?'

Blake sighed, thinking of the King's most loyal subject, Thomas Wentworth, the Earl of Strafford, the strongest man in his Privy Council. He had been sent to rule Ireland, which had been troubled by constant rebellions, but his bold and masterful methods for bringing the country to a better state had made him countless enemies in both Ireland and England.

His aim was to make the King all powerful in that country, to show both Catholics and Protestants that they must depend on the King's power, which had deepened the hatred the leaders of Parliament already felt for him—especially the all-powerful John Pym, the leader of the house and prominent opponent of the King.

'I fear so,' he said in reply to Matilda's question. 'The leaders of Parliament are set on it. After two weeks the trial did collapse and it looked like victory for Strafford—but Pym has introduced into the Commons a Bill of Attainder which simply states that Strafford is guilty and should be put to death.'

'What is it—this Bill of Attainder?' asked Matilda, who had not the slightest understanding of politics.

'It means, Matilda, that the Earl of Strafford's crime does not come under the recognition of any law or statute, so a new one has been made,' explained Blake patiently.

'And having been passed in the Commons, will the Bill pass the Lords and the King?' asked his stepmother.

'I believe it will. The pressure will be too great for them to resist.'

'Do you think he should lose his head, Blake?' asked Matilda.

'No. There is no doubt he has acted like a harsh tyrant, but nothing he has done can be called treason. The strongest charge against him—that he suggested bringing over an Irish army to subdue England—cannot be proved and is probably untrue. My belief is that it was to help quell the rebellion in Scotland.

'His trial has virtually monopolised the nation for weeks now—deflecting discontent away from the King. Strafford is a scapegoat. He has been chosen to carry the sins of the past on his shoulders as well as be an excuse for those in the future. Everyone believes that once his head has been removed then the country will run smoothly.'

'And what do you think, my lord?' asked Katherine, finding her tongue. She had listened to Blake air his views with some interest. 'Will the King live happily ever after with his subjects once Strafford is dead?'

'No,' he answered, meeting her gaze directly, pleased to see he had captured her interest. 'More than likely there will be a period of calm while the King tries to woo Parliament—but it will not last. I feel there are perilous days ahead.'

'Then why are you taking Katherine to London?' persisted Matilda, who did not begrudge Katherine this chance of going to the city but she would miss her sorely. Besides, she had no wish to be left alone at Ludgrove Hall. 'Surely she will be safer here?'

Blake continued to look at Katherine. 'Strafford's trial will soon be over and affairs at Court will return to normal for a while. You will stay away until that time. It will then be arranged for you to be presented to the King and Queen.'

Katherine wasn't thinking of the honour of this future occasion, only the relief she would feel at no longer being under her aunt's dominance.

'Oh, Katherine, you will have to have a new wardrobe,' gasped Matilda in a rush of excitement, hoping she would be able to assist in the choosing of the sumptious garments she would most certainly need to wear at Court.

'Most of what Katherine already has will be perfectly suitable,' said her mother sharply. 'Anything else she needs Amelia will see to when she reaches London. Which reminds me,' she said rising, 'I am expecting the seamstress shortly to measure you for two new gowns. Come, Matilda.'

As Katherine was about to rise and follow them Blake spoke, reluctant to let her go. Besides, if he was to take her to London then they should at least try to get on with each other.

'Do you need to hurry away also, Mistress Blair?' he said as his stepmother, with Matilda in tow, disappeared out of the room. 'Does my presence offend you so much that you have to hurry away whenever you find yourself alone with me?'

Katherine looked at him, startled. How could he accuse her of avoiding him when he was the one who had deliberately distanced himself from her?

'I was not aware that I did,' she answered stiffly.

'I have apologised for my ungentlemanly behaviour on the last occasion we found ourselves alone. I had hoped I was forgiven?' he said, smiling slowly.

Taken completely by surprise that he should refer to the incident, Katherine sank back into her seat, an embarrassed flush covering her cheeks at the rush of memory. How could he remain so calm and unconcerned as to mention something that had meant so much to her? But that he had spoken in such a casual, matter-of-fact way confirmed her fears that he cared little for her after all. Since his kiss she had dreamed of little else.

Fearing that he should guess her thoughts, she

lowered her eyes, afraid to meet his penetrating gaze
lest he should lay bare the hopeless love she carried
for him in her heart. But she was angry at herself,
angry that she could have succumbed so easily to the
embrace of this hard and unfeeling man. In control
of her feelings again, she looked across at where he
lounged indolently in his chair, watching her like a
cat watching a mouse, waiting patiently with faint
amusement for her reaction to his question.

Katherine smiled at him sweetly. 'Having heard of
your exploits where ladies are concerned, my lord,
your behaviour came as no surprise to me. And as
for apologies—well—it is a little late in the day to
withdraw what happened, don't you think? However—you may set your mind at rest. You are
forgiven. My memory of the incident is extremely
hazy. As far as I am concerned, it never happened.'

Blake gave a laugh of unbridled amusement,
doubting the truth of her statement. 'Your generosity embarrasses me, Mistress Blair. Indeed it does.'

His amusement irked Katherine somewhat, but
she continued to smile softly. 'I would not have
believed a man of your phlegmatic character capable
of embarrassment, my lord,' she said with a hint of
sarcasm.

'By that I take it that you mean I am not easily
excitable—dispassionate, even.' His eyes narrowed
and glittered meaningfully and his voice softened.
'Oh, come now—after what occurred between us the

last time we found ourselves alone together, I think you know me better than that.'

A silence fell between them, broken only by the yawning of one of the hounds at Blake's feet. His dark eyes remained fixed on Katherine's face with just the trace of a smile. It was he who broke the silence, caressing the silken ears of the dog that had raised its head and placed it in his master's lap.

'So, Mistress Blair, is Matilda right?' he asked indolently. 'Do you consider it might be too dangerous for you in London?'

'Should that be the case then I doubt you would have agreed to my going—unless, of course, my aunt is so desperate to have me gone from here that she cares not one way or the other. That I find—or purchase—a husband is all important to her whatever the case may be.'

'Make of it what you will but what you take to your husband will be the customary—and if I might say so, in your case—somewhat generous dowry. But purchase? No.'

'That's how it seems to me.'

'Clearly. But you can rest assured that I shall do my best to find you a most suitable husband.'

'I am grateful to you, my lord,' she said with an ingratiating smile, 'but if I am to marry then I shall marry a man of my own choosing.'

'Oh, yes. One you can love.' His lips twisted with sarcasm. 'I remember you saying.'

'My heart is set on it. I shall not surrender tamely

to any other. I would as soon cross to the Continent and enter a nunnery.'

Blake frowned and his expression became grave and serious. 'You are not destined to wear the habit of a nun. The Court of King Charles is a very alluring place to someone as lovely as you, Mistress Blair. There are many eligible young gallants there handsome enough to turn your head.'

Katherine stared at him with frank amazement. Never had she thought to hear such a compliment pass his lips. 'Handsome enough—I do not doubt. Rich enough I do.'

Blake's eyes narrowed. 'So—you would have your eyes on a fortune after all?'

'No. But neither am I so stupid or naïve as to fall at the feet of the first handsome gentleman who makes eyes at me, my lord, such as Sir George Carrington or Lord Forbes, seeing not myself but the fortune I carry as a means of paying off his debts. I would rather not marry at all, if that be the case.'

'But if you should fall in love?' Blake murmured softly, speaking slowly, his eyes never leaving hers for a moment. 'What will you give then?'

His voice reached out to her and held her. She looked at him enquiringly, her eyes held by his. There was something in their depths, in the way he was looking at her which seemed to convey a message, and it was a moment so momentous as not to be broken. At length she managed to answer.

'Everything. It's as simple as that.' She rose to her

feet, lowering her eyes over the flush on her cheeks. 'Pray excuse me, my lord. I must see if the seamstress has arrived. I promised to assist her in measuring Matilda up for her new gowns.'

'Of course,' said Blake, also rising. 'Run along. I did not mean to detain you.'

He watched her go out of the room before seating himself again, frowning at the closed door, deep in thought, the silence broken only by the sound of her footsteps becoming fainter on the stone flags in the passage outside.

CHAPTER FIVE

AFTER all the packing had been done, Katherine had been ready to leave for London, optimistic that she would enjoy being away from her aunt and with Amelia. Her maid, Rose, had accompanied her. Blake was to have travelled inside the coach with them—although for most of the journey, having been disturbed by Katherine's close proximity, he had escaped the confines of the interior, having preferred to sit up front with the driver.

He had considered taking one of his own horses but, on reflection, had decided against it, for there would be plenty of mounts to choose from at Landale House. Amelia's husband prided himself on his stables.

It had been a tearful Matilda that Katherine had said goodbye to. She had felt sorry to be leaving her, wishing that she'd been allowed to come too. Doubtless, by the time she returned to Ludgrove Hall her aunt would have succeeded in finding Matilda a suitor.

The journey to London had been uneventful and it was with relief that they arrived at Landale House. The Earl of Landale had recently moved from his house close to Westminster and the river—from the

smoke and soot-grimed buildings, the overcrowd-
ing and congestion of the streets—to the more
wholesome, fashionable atmosphere of Covent
Garden where new houses were being built and
where people of social eminence were beginning to
live.

Despite the authoritative sobriety of the Court of
King Charles, Amelia was an extremely popular and
sought-after figure, her title as the Countess of
Landale giving her access to the Court. She surrounded herself with luxuries and enjoyed a lavish
lifestyle, throwing herself into all the activities at
Court, never missing a ball or a masque—of which
the Queen was particularly fond—or going to see
the opening of a new play at the theatre. She often
stayed in rooms at Whitehall or threw supper parties
at Landale House, entertaining on a grand scale.
Her husband George, the mild-mannered Earl of
Landale, gave her free rein to do as she wished.

Katherine was immediately enthralled and excited
by it all—unlike Blake, who frowned with abject
distaste at what he considered to be his sister's
wanton extravagance, and was beginning to distrust
the influence she would have over the naïve
Katherine. But there was little he could do about
that now. He could hardly return her to her aunt, so
he became determined to set about finding her a
husband immediately—although he already had a
young man in mind who might prove to be suitable.

Amelia frowned on Katherine's wardrobe, which

her aunt had pronounced suitable but which Amelia cast aside with distaste, commenting that her dowdy and uninteresting clothes might be suitable for the country but not for the Court. She immediately whisked her off to the Exchange on the Strand where she set about having her fitted for a whole new wardrobe.

During her early days in London, her mother and brother were never out of Katherine's thoughts for long and she yearned for the time when she could discover what had become of them.

She saw little of Blake. His time was spent at the London residence of the Earl of Rockley in the company of Lady Margaret, and at the warehouses and wharves where he was overseeing the unloading and storing of a cargo of tobacco from one of his ships that had just arrived from the West Indies, and where he was also busy arranging contracts for the ship's next voyage and fulfilling the plantation owners' orders for European goods.

As London awaited the outcome of the Earl of Strafford's trial there was a nervous unease about the city. The Commons had passed Pym's Bill of Attainder but now it faced two higher hurdles—the Lords and the King. If the Bill passed the Lords, what would the King do? everyone was asking. Like any other Bill, it was subject to the King's assent. The King owed much to Strafford and had promised him he would never consent to his execution, but could he weather the storm of maddened, uncontrollable crowds besieging Whitehall and Westminster demanding Strafford's head?

Unable to have Katherine presented at Court because of the present troubles, Amelia had been busy arranging other activities, like supper parties and visits to the theatre. She even managed to coax Blake, on one of his rare moments of inactivity, into escorting them on an outing in Hyde Park. Her own husband had temporarily left London for his estate in Kent.

The park, which sported two bowling greens and where horse racing took place and dairy maids walked round with fresh creamy milk for the thirsty, was a rendezvous of fashion and beauty. Where anyone with a splendid equipage went to see and be seen. Blue skies spilled sunlight onto the many courtiers out to make the most of it, in open carriages with impressive coats of arms emblazoned on doors, and handsome young bucks prancing along the pathways on superb horse flesh.

Ladies were dressed in full splendour, their hats trimmed with delicate, tantalising plumes and tied with satin ribbons. Katherine sat beside Amelia in the carriage while Blake rode alongside, cutting a dashing figure on a big bay stallion, attracting many raised eyebrows and admiring, languishing feminine glances from behind unfurled fans—none of which were lost on Katherine. Amelia had seen to it that

Katherine's saffron coloured costume was as grand as any in the park.

It was when Blake had stopped to speak to an acquaintance, falling some distance behind, that a man boldly rode towards them, pulling on the reins and stopping his horse beside their carriage, which had paused by a flowered border to wait for Blake. Katherine was so absorbed with trying to take in the names of everyone of note whom Amelia pointed out that she failed to notice him until she looked round and recognised Lord Forbes. At first she was as startled as if she had seen a ghost.

'Why—my dear Mistress Blair!' he said, smiling broadly and removing his wide-brimmed hat from his pale blond locks. 'So it is you. At first I thought I must be dreaming. How good it is to see you again.'

Katherine stared at him. The memory of their last meeting made her cheeks flush with embarrassment but, recollecting the humiliation she had suffered at his hands, her spine stiffened and she gave him a cold stare.

'Lord Forbes! I do not know how you have the audacity to face me, let alone speak to me after what transpired on our last meeting.'

'I know I have fallen into disfavour and I wouldn't blame you if you refused to speak to me. You may not believe this but I still feel wretched about the way I treated you. My conduct was quite inexcusable.'

It was the kind of graceful remark any gentleman

would have made under such circumstances but Katherine could not help feeling that he did not mean a word of it. His face had taken on an expression of self-reproach but there was a hint of mischief sparkling in his hooded eyes.

'Yes—it was, indeed,' she replied.

'I have thought about you often, Mistress Blair, and wondered if you could ever find it in your heart to forgive me?'

'Forgive you? What? After the way you tried to degrade me, how can I possibly forgive you?'

'Please believe me when I say it was not my intention to degrade you in any way. Oh, come now,' he almost begged, 'can we not call a truce?' His face suddenly broke into an impudent smile, his eyes appraising her warmly, and clearly he felt no shame for his actions of that night at the inn.

Katherine would have liked to remain cool and composed but his smile was infectious and irresistible. In spite of herself, her irritation fell away and she could not resist returning his smile—to Amelia's shock and deep displeasure.

'You are extremely persuasive, Lord Forbes.'

'So—I am forgiven?'

Katherine hesitated but, believing him to be sincere—although no matter how friendly he became she would always have cause to mistrust him—finally she nodded, which made his smile widen.

'You have made me a very happy man, Mistress Blair. I'm not so bad, you know, but at the inn that night, on finding myself alone with you, I quite lost my head. You bowled me over. There—I have admitted it.'

'Dear me!' Katherine exclaimed, bursting out laughing. 'Your impudence knows no bounds. You are incorrigible, sir. But I must tell you that I do not return the sentiment. Oh,' she said, remembering her manners and turning to Amelia. 'May I present the Countess of Landale. I'm staying with her for a while.'

Amelia bridled when Lord Forbes's eyes came to rest on her and she did not miss the icy glint in their depths.

'Lord Forbes and I are already acquainted, Katherine,' she said, fixing him with a cold stare. 'But I do not believe you are aware that Lord Russell is my brother, Lord Forbes. Knowing of his antagonism towards you, you would be wise to ride on this instant before he sees you and demands to finish the business you started, before you left the inn like a scared rabbit with the pack hot on your tail.'

Glancing back along the path, an uneasy expression crossed Lord Forbes's face for he could see Lord Russell was already looking towards the carriage. He turned and smiled once more at Katherine. 'I'm happy to see your aunt didn't force you into marriage with old Sir George. What a waste that would have been.'

'Believing me to be despoiled, Lord Forbes,'

Katherine replied drily, 'Sir George would not have me.'

'Then methinks you have much to thank me for, Mistress Blair. I did you a favour.'

'One I shall not return, Lord Forbes,' she replied, fixing him with a steady gaze.

'I would not presume,' he purred. 'However, I am grateful that you spared the time to speak to me. If I can be of service to you—please do not hesitate to ask. I'll see you again, I hope,' he said, addressing Katherine.

'Not if my brother has anything to do with it. Good day, Lord Forbes,' said Amelia, dismissing him abruptly.

Still smiling broadly, Lord Forbes bowed and rode away.

'Really,' she gasped, 'the cheek of the man—and as smooth as ever.' She cast Katherine a glance of exasperation. 'And you, Katherine. Why—sometimes I worry about you—truly I do. Your nature is too forgiving. You are too easily won over. After what that blackguard did to you you should have ignored him completely.'

Katherine smiled at Amelia. 'I know, but you cannot deny that there is something charismatically appealing about him, Amelia. Besides—he was pleasantly civil.'

Amelia drew in a sharp breath. 'So he should be. He's had plenty of practice. Don't be deceived by his honeyed voice and drooping eyes, Katherine. He has a lying, flattering tongue and spends his time prowling the galleries of Whitehall and the drawing-rooms of London's élite in search of an heiress.

'Women without means swoon at the sight of his fair locks and his elegance. They fall for him like dominoes in a row, but when they get to know him they change their tune. Anyone with any sense at all will have nothing to do with him. You already know him for the vile seducer he is. He's been the cause of many an open scandal, and why—he almost succeeded where you were concerned. Don't be fool enough to fall for his charming allure a second time.'

Katherine laughed lightly. 'What a simpleton you must take me for, Amelia. Rest assured—I know Lord Forbes for what he is and shall not be duped again.'

'I sincerely hope not—for, mark my words, whatever happened between the two of you at the inn that night hasn't changed a thing where he is concerned. It would be a coup indeed if he were to win your hand.'

'Don't worry, I shall keep my wits about me at all times. I promise. But he did seem genuinely sincere in wanting to make amends.'

'To you, maybe, but I very much doubt it—and I doubt Blake will see it that way, either. I only hope he did not see him talking to you for there will be the devil to pay.'

Blake had seen—and also the smile on Katherine's face as she conversed with Lord Forbes. Anger at her stupidity rose inside him. Excusing himself to his acquaintance, he rode quickly away in the hope of accosting him, but the wily knave had seen him advancing towards the carriage and quickly disappeared into the crowd. Blake's face was like thunder when he looked at Katherine, who was still smiling softly, adding fuel to his rage.

'Did my eyes deceive me or was that that reprobate Lord Forbes I saw you conversing with so happily?'

The smile disappeared from Katherine's lips and she scowled up at him. 'You may rest assured, my lord, there is nothing wrong with your eyes. It was Lord Forbes—apologising most sincerely for his unseemly conduct on our last meeting.'

'And like a naïve little fool you believed him,' he growled.

Blake's eyes shifted to where Amelia sat, eyeing him nervously. She was well accustomed to her brother's fits of temper and usually stood up to him, but this time she knew better than to argue—unlike Katherine, who glared at him. 'And you, Amelia,' he continued, 'should have known better than to allow him to approach the carriage.'

'It was not Amelia's fault,' flared Katherine, coming quickly to her defence, Blake's readiness to blame his sister making her furious. 'Lord Forbes was upon us before we could do anything about it.'

'And by the simpering look on your face you

accommodated him readily enough. You know as well as I what is in his mind.'

'Ha,' Katherine scoffed. 'The same that is in the minds of most men, I should think.'

Blake's eyes narrowed dangerously and his expression became venomous, but he chose to ignore her remark. 'I object to the way you made a display of yourself, for there are few here in the park today who are not aware of what took place between the two of you the last time you met. Was not his attempt then to ruin you enough? By accepting his apologies so readily then, mark my words, he'll continue his pursuit of you.'

Katherine's eyes flamed rebelliously. 'Owing to your own past experiences, my lord, you are extremely quick to suspect the worst.'

'Oh—do stop it, you two,' Amelia burst in. 'Do you have to argue here in the park—making a spectacle of us all? See—people are beginning to stare.'

'You are right,' Blake replied, observing the glittering, gossiping passers-by looking their way. 'Come, it is time we returned to the house.'

Angry that her first outing to the park was to end so abruptly, for an instant Katherine almost voiced the protest that rose to her lips, but on seeing the grim set of Blake's countenance, forbidding any further argument, she did not dare. She merely threw him a sullen glare and turned her head away.

* * *

The House of Lords had passed the Bill of Attainder on the Earl of Strafford, leaving the final decision as to his fate up to the King. Ugly mobs had besieged the palace, howling for justice and Strafford's head, threatening to storm it if their wishes were not met. This had been the King's darkest hour and the terror that had gripped him in his misery had been real. At last, fearing for the safety of his family, especially that of his beloved Catholic Queen, who would hardly survive if the maddened mob broke the barriers of the palace walls, he had agreed to the execution.

Amid the celebrations of the marriage of William of Orange and Princess Mary, the King's eldest daughter, there had still prevailed an undercurrent of unrest within the city. Riots and demonstrations against the King and all he stood for were an everyday occurrence. But, as Blake had predicted, now that Strafford was dead, the pressure surrounding the King and Queen had relaxed, although the troubles were far from over. Storm clouds were again gathering to the north with Scotland.

Blake's dark eyes were increasingly troubled. He was deeply concerned not only with what was happening to the country, but even more so with what was happening between the King and his Parliament.

With rare discretion Katherine had tried hard to please Blake. Since the unfortunate incident in the park, once his anger over her tardy respect for her pride had abated, surprisingly, he had become more

civil towards her. The softening in his eyes had made
her believe that maybe he was beginning to warm to
her.

On returning from the docks one day, Blake was
greeted in the hallway of Landale House by a loud
cacophony of feminine chattering and laughter
coming from the upper floors of the house. He did
not wonder at the cause of such feverish merriment
and excitement. Today Katherine was to make her
début at Court. He heard the sound of her laughter,
which rang in his ears and seemed to fill the whole
house, a sound all the sweeter because of its rarity.

He looked up the stairs, totally unprepared for the
sight his eyes beheld. At that moment Katherine
appeared before him like a mirage rising out of the
desert, tall and beautiful—not the innocent beauty
of yesterday, for that had been without art, without
the glittering jewels that adorned her throat and
hung from her ears like droplets of sparkling water,
halted in its flow.

Now the expertise of the dressmaker and hair-
dresser had changed her. She had been lovely
before—now she was glorious. The gown she wore
was of cloth of gold, covered with a deeper delicate
gold lace, the same colour as her hair.

Managing to conquer a traitorous rush of tenderness, Blake moved out of the gloom and into the
light cast from the large windows, knowing that,
looking as she did, she would be sure to fire the

blood of many of the courtiers. With this thought in mind he was determined to introduce her; to Lord Soames, the young gentleman of good breeding and sufficient means whom he intended her to marry, without delay, and who would take her away to his country seat in Devon.

Unaware of Blake's thoughts, which would not have pleased her, Katherine stared down at him with some surprise for she had seen little of him of late. Excited at the prospect of going to Whitehall at last, her eyes sparkled and a happy smile hovered on her lips—as Amelia's ladies had dressed her, all the while she had been thinking of Blake and that she was dressing for him alone.

She felt so happy and elated that not even the prospect of meeting Lady Margaret Tawney once again was allowed to cloud her day. With her heart beating like a drum, lifting her skirts slightly to reveal the velvet toes of her slippered feet, she descended the stairs, seeming to glide over the polished wood floor. She paused in front of him, her blue eyes wide as they gazed into his, aware of the change he must see in her.

'So, my lord, your presence here at this time of the day surprises me. I would have thought you had much to occupy your time at the wharves.'

'My business for today is concluded. I have not forgotten that it is today you are to be presented at Court and—if I may say so,' he said softly, breathing in the sweet, heady scent of apple blossom, 'you look

exquisite. Not even the Queen will be able to out-
shine you looking as you do.'

For a moment there was a flash of genuine feeling
in his eyes as they raked Katherine from head to toe,
the first expression of true appraisal she had ever
seen on his face, causing her heart to swell with love
and hope, giving her a buoyant sensation. She looked
at him, wide-eyed. His hair was untidy, his face lined
faintly with fatigue, his jacket and breeches stained
from his work at the docks, his wide-topped boots
and spurs dusty—still the sight of him did not fail to
stir her heart.

She was tempted to reply—What? Not even Lady
Margaret? but thought better of it, not wishing to
sound malicious or ungracious. 'Why—I thank you,
my lord,' she replied instead, delighting that she had
succeeded in winning his admiration. She suddenly
felt so bold that she dared to let a faint provocative
smile touch the corners of her mouth and she gave
him a sidelong look from under her lashes. 'A
compliment from you is a rarity indeed.'

If she had hoped for further appraisal from him
then she was to be disappointed for, undeceived, her
coquettish air found no favour with Blake, who
frowned with disapproval.

'Doubtless there will be many eager young gallants falling over themselves to pay tribute to your
beauty at Whitehall, all too ready with their compliments today and in the days to come. But do not
play the coquette with me, Mistress Blair. The role

does not become you—and I know you too well. I have never been one to indulge in the meaningless plaudits which seem to be all the fashion at Court.'

The unexpected harshness of his words caused Katherine's eyes to open wide with genuine amazement and innocence. 'Why—I am sure I do not know what you mean.'

No, thought Blake, she truly had no idea. But he refused to let himself be swayed from the course he had set himself where she was concerned by explaining. His heart softened but his expression remained hard.

'I think my meaning is plain enough. The excitement of going to Whitehall, combined with the glitter you imagine you will find there, has made you realise the effect your beauty will have on the male members of the Court. It may have temporarily slipped your mind but I am betrothed to Lady Margaret, so do not count me as one of them.'

Katherine scowled up at him, indignant at the slight. 'You flatter yourself unduly, my lord, if you think that—and no, it has not slipped my mind that you are to marry Lady Margaret. I look forward to making her acquaintance once again, but in my opinion I cannot help but think that some time spent at Court—with its reputation for orderliness and ceremony might well improve your manners.'

Blake's lips twisted with irony. 'I lay little store by what happens at Court, which reeks of the Vatican. There's more to life than having to spend it with

knaves and fools—with little else to do but become
embroiled in intrigue—all plotting and scheming
against each other and fawning around the King for
favours unearned.'

Katherine's heart had contracted painfully at his
reference to the Vatican, reminding her of her
mother and his aversion to the Catholic faith, but
she gave no indication of this. 'Then what do you
want from life, my lord?'

'What I want is unimportant for the present. It is
what England will ask of me and every other
Englishman that matters—whatever I might think.'

His voice had become quiet, his expression grave,
and his eyes looked past Katherine as they journeyed
ahead of her into the future. She knew he was
thinking of the troubles that beset the country, which
in all probability was fast tumbling into a situation
that would result in civil war. She thrust these ugly
thoughts from her mind for they were too fearful to
contemplate at this time.

'Meanwhile,' Blake continued, 'I would be obliged
if you would save your flirtations for someone who
is available and more gullible. In the absence of the
Earl of Landale, who is more familiar with the Court
than myself and whom I had hoped would present
you to the King and Queen because I have been too
long away, I shall escort you to Whitehall myself.'

Katherine flushed, realising that her silly attempt
to flirt with him had been treated with the contempt
he would have accorded someone of no account.

Inwardly raging at his ability to read her mind, and shocked at her own transparency, she drew in a sharp breath and would dearly have loved to turn on her heel and tell him to go to the devil, that she would go to Whitehall without him or not at all.

But pride and the cold hand of common-sense prevailed. After all, she could hardly present herself at Court and she did so want him to be with her. Swallowing her anger she assumed an expression of pleasant dignity and again smiled up at him.

'As you wish,' she murmured sweetly. 'But,' she said, wrinkling her nose with distaste, 'I have to say that your apparel is more in keeping with the docks than the elegance of Whitehall.'

'Which can soon be rectified. I left instructions for my valet to have my clothes in readyness for when I returned. So—if you will excuse me I shall go and change.'

CHAPTER SIX

FILLED with excitement and happiness at being escorted to Whitehall Palace by Blake, Katherine sat opposite him in the carriage with Amelia beside her, whose ladies were following on in another carriage. She sat straight backed, staring at everything she saw out of the window as they travelled along the Strand of this centuries-old city, its skyline peppered with innumerable church spires. The city was attractive, repelling and fascinating all at once, its vitality springing from a variety of commerce and industry within its walls. It was vibrant and violent, thriving and alive, the centre of England and, as far as Katherine was concerned, the whole universe. It stirred her deepest emotions and she never ceased to be enthralled by it all.

Within London's walls the conglomeration of muddled and unplanned narrow streets, abounding with beggars and footpads, were like a rabbit warren; a mixture of splendour and squalor, dark, dirty and ugly, often running with filth and the air reeking with the stench of decaying refuse, and yet at the same time possessing a rotten kind of beauty, colourful and noisy, with street vendors and rowdy markets to which people came from all over the surrounding countryside in droves to sell their produce. There was a marked contrast between the residences of the rich and poor, and when one reached the rich men's homes that lined the Strand and the royal palaces which stretched along the river front from Whitehall to the mouth of the Fleet, the squalid hovels of the not so privileged were less frequent.

They reached Whitehall Palace, a huge sprawling mass of buildings to the west of the city, the chief residence of the Court. It was a labyrinth of streets and alleyways, of apartments inhabited by noblemen and armies of their dependents. Through its middle ran the narrow thoroughfare of King Street, the north side of the Palace housing the cockpit and tennis courts and the tiltyard where tournaments and bear baiting were held.

Usually anyone who had anything to do with the Court could enter and wander about at will, but because of the present riots and the threat to the King's person, security at the gates was tight. They entered through the Palace Gate; inside there was great bustle with lackeys and footmen in a multitude of coloured liveries flitting about all over the place. Blake escorted Katherine and Amelia, followed by a chattering group of her ladies, up the stairs to the long Stone Gallery. Katherine gazed about her rapt with enchantment, for never had her eyes beheld anything as splendid. From what she knew of King Charles's Court it was said to be the abode of elegance and learning, of purity and refinement, where culture flourished, but upon seeing it for the first time she knew it to be also a place of great beauty, where bejewelled ladies shimmered in satined gowns.

'Well?' asked Blake, watching Katherine's reaction to the scene with interest. 'Are you impressed?'

'Most certainly,' she gasped with wide-eyed wonder, thrilled by the splendour of it all. 'How beautiful it all is—and so many people. Where do they all come from?'

'All over England and the Continent. Are you all right?' he asked suddenly with measured concern and a genuine desire for her well-being, sensing the strain lurking beneath the glow on her face.

She gave him a shaky smile. 'If you must know, I'm terribly nervous.'

Blake smiled down at her reassuringly. 'Then don't be. The King will be charmed by you—as will every other courtier here today when they see you. There's nothing like a new face at Court—especially a beautiful one—to set tongues wagging. Although, compared to the rumbustiousness of his father's Court, many find the Court of King Charles rather dull. There are few drunken brawls or spicy scandals but there are still a certain amount of profligate characters who hang around, nevertheless. Come—let's move on.'

Gently but firmly taking her arm, Blake escorted her through the throng. Katherine was grateful to him for the way he tried to put her at her ease and she wondered when she would meet his betrothed. Was Lady Margaret already there—somewhere in the crowd waiting for him to arrive?

Katherine was eager and full of admiration for everything she saw, her eyes darting about so as not to miss a thing, becoming very much aware of the attention Blake was attracting from the ladies present—although he appeared not to notice.

The walls on either side of the gallery were embellished with carefully chosen works of art, some by the Italian masters Titian and Raphael, which spoke of the King's own excellent taste and his love of art. They were just a few of the superb collection he had accumulated over the years.

After leaving the gallery, they entered the King's presence chamber which was packed with courtiers and where presentations were already taking place. Even from the gilded doorway Katherine had no difficulty in distinguishing the figure of the King, with the Queen by his side, seated on a dais. Katherine was a little disappointed at her first sighting of him, for seeing him in the flesh he did not live up to the larger-than-life image she had built of him in her mind, but as she moved closer she became aware that, though he must be slight in stature when standing, his majesty was undiminished.

The King was exchanging jovial words with those who surrounded him. Blake and his party were announced by a court usher and as he drew Katherine forward the King looked towards them, as did the courtiers who surrounded him. The presentations almost over, ignoring ceremony, the King rose, stepping down from the dais and moving forward to greet Blake, for whom he had a particular liking and who had been absent from his Court for some considerable time.

'Why, Lord Russell, it is good to see you among us once again. My Court has been noticeably poorer by your absence.'

'My apologies, Sire,' Blake replied bowing low, unphased at being in the King's presence, 'but owing to the death of my father since my return from the Indies, matters have kept me in Appleby.'

The King's expression became grave; he'd had great respect for the old Lord Russell, a scholarly man of sound judgement—though with little interest in politics.

'My commiserations. Your father will be sorely missed. He brought us joy and we loved him well. I, for one, valued his sound common-sense and views and opinions greatly. I hope you are to remain in London for a while and to take your seat in the Lords vacated by your father. Although,' he said, smiling wryly though speaking not unkindly, 'I always felt he had little interest in matters of state, preferring instead to be embroiled in his mercantile business or estate matters in Appleby. Although— when one considers the state of the nation—ah, well—who can blame him?' he said, sighing deeply.

Blake smiled. 'There is much truth in what you

say, Sire. My father liked nothing better than organising his ships as he did his estate. As for myself, I hope to take my seat in the Lords in due course.'

'I'm glad to hear it—and I must congratulate you on your forthcoming marriage to Lady Margaret Tawney. A fair maid indeed.' His eyes shifted with interest to the still figure of Katherine by his side. 'And who is this, pray? Can it be the young lady we have heard much about from Countess Landale? Who, I might add, has sung your praises to the Queen ever since your arrival in London.'

'Sire—may I have the honour of presenting to you Mistress Blair—the ward of Lady Harriet Russell, her aunt and my stepmother,' said Blake, his dark gaze falling on Katherine as he drew her forward.

Lowering her eyes, Katherine sank into a deep curtsy, feeling more nervous than she had ever felt in her life. Her legs were trembling so much—as were her hands, encased in elbow-length gloves, tucked into the folds of her dress. Managing to rise with dignity, she hardly dared to breathe as she gazed at King Charles with awe and respect, feeling all the eyes in the room converge on her.

There was an abiding air of sadness about him. Blake had told her he mourned the passing of the Earl of Strafford deeply and that he was haunted by him but, deep though his sorrow was, he would have to overcome it to give attention to the important matters of state that pressed heavily on his shoulders.

'Mistress Blair is a welcome addition to the Court,

Lord Russell—and, moreover, a most beautiful one. Take care, my dear,' he said softly, his eyes twinkling good humouredly, 'for I fear your arrival among us will set many a masculine heart beating to distraction. But I daresay that under the firm guidance and protection of Lord Russell I'm sure you'll have little trouble in keeping any unwanted amorous advances at bay.'

Katherine dared to cast a sideways look at Blake who was completely at his ease and was looking at her with some amusement. She looked back at the King, captivated by his dark eyes and warm effortless charm, feeling some of her nervousness evaporate. She smiled, flushing softly, wishing that the only amorous advances she would be likely to procure would be from Blake himself.

'Yes, I'm sure you're right, Sire.'

'Your arrival among us is bound to cause a sensation—but do not be taken in for the greater a lady's popularity with the gentlemen of the Court the quicker the other ladies' venom rises. Is that not so, Lord Russell?' chuckled the King, giving Blake a sidelong conspiratorial look which caused him to laugh outright with genuine amusement, the King's words holding some secret meaning known only to those familiar with the ways of the Court.

'Indeed it is, Sire,' Blake replied, 'as many have found out to their cost.'

'Tell me, Mistress Blair, are you from Warwickshire?'

'No, Sire. My family is from the north—although my childhood was spent in Kent with my father.'

'I have known Mistress Blair since she was ten years old, Sire,' explained Blake. 'Upon the death of her father she was made her aunt's ward and came to live with us at Ludgrove Hall where she was brought up with my younger brother and sister.'

The King bowed his head slightly. 'My Court is very happy to receive you, Mistress Blair.' He turned to the Queen whose attention had been drawn to the beautiful girl with the golden hair being presented to her husband. 'Madam, may I present Mistress Blair, the ward of Lady Harriet Russell?'

Queen Henrietta Maria, in a crimson gown, her dark shining curls threaded through with a rope of pearls framing a small face with large, brilliant dark eyes and an ivory quality to her skin, bestowed a charming smile on Katherine who felt a flickering of admiration for this Catholic queen who, despite the trials and tribulations of the past months and the loss of her three year-old-daughter at the end of the previous year, still managed to look adversity in the eye. Katherine sank into another deep curtsy.

'So—you are Mistress Blair. We've heard a great deal about you from Countess Landale,' said the Queen. Her voice held a heavy trace of her French accent that added to its charm. She beckoned to Amelia who had come to stand among her group of ladies. 'You did not exaggerate, Countess. Mistress Blair is fair indeed. If you feel so inclined,' she said, again addressing Katherine, 'come with Countess Landale and visit us at Somerset House. You will be most welcome.'

'Thank you. Your Majesty is too kind,' said Katherine rising .

Katherine stepped back as the Queen and Amelia continued to converse. The words that passed between them appeared to be formal banalities, but to Katherine, looking on, it had the appearance of being a relaxed conversation between established friends.

The presentations over, the King took Blake to one side, speaking at length of his late father and how matters fared with the Western Trading Company during this depression. Katherine stood aside for so enraptured was she at being in this magical place with Blake that she was content to let her eyes dwell on him, thinking how handsome he looked in his violet suit with his dark hair falling heavily to his broad shoulders. Beside him, every man in the room paled into insignificance.

How easily he conversed with the King—so sure of himself—so utterly confident. She noticed how his eyes would occasionally sweep the room and a heaviness descended on her heart; no doubt he was searching for Lady Margaret who did not seem to have arrived yet. But then his eyes would meet hers and he would smile with an unusually warm intimacy which made her volatile spirit soar with happiness.

At that moment she loved him so much it was like a deep physical pain.

That every lady in the room was enamoured of Blake was evident from the way they were gazing at him—some with starry eyes and others like hungry wolves, and they stared at her with such open curiosity as to be almost rude.

Oh, she thought wistfully, if only she were his intended instead of Lady Margaret. Wouldn't that give them all something to gossip about? The very idea gave her a heady sense of dizziness, and a powerful longing, to feel his arms about her and the thrill of his lips on hers once again, swept over her. She was brought abruptly out of her dreamy state when Amelia claimed her, sweeping her away to introduce her to her friends.

After a while and quite unexpectedly, Katherine became aware of an attractive, foreign-looking nobleman not twelve feet away from her. Casually her eyes passed on to his companion. Her attention was drawn to him because he was dressed in the sombre black garments of a cleric, yet seemed to be watching her closely. He had a pleasant countenance and a shock of bright blond hair. Not wishing to stare, she turned away; feeling his eyes still on her, she turned and looked at him again, her bold stare meeting his blue, somewhat inquisitive, eyes.

He was quite tall and of slender build and, she thought, in his early twenties. At first sight there was nothing out of the ordinary about him—he was a

priest like any other. As she was about to turn away
again, suddenly something familiar stirred in her
memory, taking her back over several weeks to
Appleby and the day when her horse had shed one
of its shoes and she had been sitting outside The
Black Boar inn sipping lemonade with Amelia,
watching the young man who had been sitting close
by reading his book.

Why, this man in the robes of a priest and the man
she had seen that day were so alike they could
almost be the same. But it could not be possible. It
was mere coincidence, that was all. But the longer
she looked into his steady, intense eyes, she began
to experience the same disquieting feeling of puzzlement as she had on that day.

He began to move away with his companion and
Katherine's eyes followed, but she was distracted
when Blake, having noticed her standing alone, her
eyes with their long shadowing lashes gazing across
the room and the interest she was showing in the
priest, came over to her. She smiled up at him, but
her eyes again sought out the young priest who was
leaving the room with his companion.

Blake frowned with irritation. 'You have a way of
gazing at Father Edmund that alarms me, Mistress
Blair,' he said quietly. 'It is most unmannerly to look
at any man with such intensity, let alone a priest.'

'Father Edmund,' she murmured. 'So that is his
name.'

'Why the interest?'

'He—he seems familiar, that is all,' she replied, still watching the priest's retreating figure.

'Familiar? How can that be?' Blake sighed crossly, annoyed that she continued to gaze after him and at his own inability to hold her interest. 'What can his fascination be, I ask myself? His looks? For he is fair, that I grant you. Or could it be the priestly mystique of his faith that draws you to him? It does many other ladies who surround the Queen.'

Having watched Father Edmund disappear from sight, Katherine once again fixed Blake with her questioning eyes, sensing his aversion to the priest.

'What have you against him?'

Blake shrugged. 'I have nothing against him personally. In fact, I know very little about Father Edmund—only that he is English by birth and has lived for some considerable time in France and Rome where he was ordained. He came to London in thirty-nine with Count Rossetti—the papal envoy to the Queen.'

Katherine looked at him sharply. 'But how is it that Father Edmund is allowed to remain when all priests have been banished from Court?' she asked curiously. 'Why, Amelia told me that foreign ambassadors of Catholic countries, fearing for their lives, have asked to be called away from England—that even the Queen has been asked to dismiss her Catholic servants.'

'Yes, that is so—and some priests have been arrested and already put to death.'

'And do you condone such punishments, my lord?' asked Katherine quietly. 'That a man should die for his beliefs? Should Catholics continue to be persecuted with the old severity as was the case in Queen Elizabeth's time?'

Blake looked down at her upturned enquiring face gravely, relieved there was no one within earshot to hear their conversation. It was dangerous to be heard speaking of so grave a matter which could be construed as plotting.

'There was a time when the open practice for Catholics at Court attracted general attention, when the Queen was surrounded by intelligent and cultivated priests. Lord knows I am not a Puritan by any means and neither am I deeply religious, but in the early days, when the King married his French Queen, when the Catholics descended on us in droves, my Protestant soul was offended and cried out to have them removed.

'I always disapproved of the freedom they were accorded at Court, distrusting the influence they had over the Queen and knowing they were taking advantage of the King's clemency to make converts. But,' he said, looking down at her seriously, 'in answer to your question, no, I do not think a man should be persecuted or put to death for what he believes in.'

'Then why does Father Edmund remain at Court?'

'That I cannot answer. He is close to Count Rossetti—that was Count Rossetti he was with. He is a private emissary sent to the Queen according to her marriage treaty. As far as I am aware Father Edmund hasn't been seen for quite some time; it was thought he might have fled the country. Odd that he should reappear today.

'Since the death of Strafford the pressure may have eased somewhat on the King and Queen—Parliament being occupied with excluding bishops from Government office—but nevertheless neither House ignores what goes on at Whitehall and both are indignant that Rossetti continues to reside in England. He will be sent back to Rome sooner rather than later, I should think.'

'And what of Father Edmund?' asked Katherine, saddened by the thought that anything dreadful should happen to him.

'He will not be accorded the same leniency. He is an Englishman and will eventually be imprisoned like the rest and—unless he takes an oath of allegiance, recognising the sovereign as the lawful and rightful king, repudiating the papal claim to depose heretical princes—he will be executed.'

On seeing the horror enter Katherine's eyes, Blake smiled reassuringly. 'He is aware of what will happen so it is up to him to do something about it before it is too late. If he has any sense and is discreet then he might be able to escape back to Rome. But,' he sighed, his dark eyes twinkling in an attempt to lighten the conversation, to draw her mind away from Father Edmund, 'to my mind it is a sin for one so fair to be shrouded in the confining robes of a priest, which forbid the pleasures we ordinary mortals take so much for granted and enjoy.'

Katherine's cheeks dimpled in a smile, wishing this rare moment of intimacy between them would never end. 'Methinks the pleasures you speak of, my lord, are of the immoral kind, without the sacred oath of fidelity which comes with marriage. No matter how fiercely you assail the Catholic faith, it proves unshakeable to those who belong. They are more to be envied than reviled. Father Edmund is a priest and has forsaken all earthly pleasures. It does not make him any less a man because of it. If that is what he wants then so be it.'

She spoke with such ardour that it had brought a gentle flush to her cheeks. Blake looked down at the seriousness in her eyes with mild amusement, thinking how lovely she was. He nodded slowly. 'Aye—so be it. What matter is it to anyone else how one chooses to live one's life?' In good humour he took her arm. 'Come. Enough talk of Father Edmund. I want to introduce you to a few people I know who are eager to meet you.'

The warm reassuring pressure of Blake's hand on her arm set Katherine's pulses racing and she floated by his side in a state of euphoria, but she could not resist one last look at the doorway through which Father Edmund had disappeared a short while before with Count Rossetti.

Her euphoria soon evaporated. Lady Margaret Tawney arrived on the arm of her father, the Earl of Rockley, who paused to speak to an acquaintance. Margaret's eyes swept the room, alighting almost instantly on Blake, whose face brightened when he saw her. Leaving her father, she threaded her way through the throng, moving towards them, a smile curving her lips.

She was smaller than Katherine, the bone structure of her face fine and delicate, and there was a certain frailty about her slender form. Katherine looked at her with some concern, thinking how ill she looked, for Margaret was much changed from what she remembered. There was a hollow, pallid aspect to her skin and she looked as if she would faint at the least exertion. But there was a quiet dignity about her which was touching and drew people to her.

Despite the fact that she was betrothed to Blake, Katherine's opinion of her had not changed. She liked her—although it would have been easier for her if she didn't—but it was difficult not to like someone who exuded so much warmth and friendliness.

When she smiled, Katherine thought how pretty she was. She noticed how Margaret's eyes lit up with an inner fire when she looked at Blake, telling the whole world that he belonged to her. It was then that Katherine saw that Lady Margaret Tawney was completely in love with the man she was to marry—

it was like a dagger thrust to the heart. What chance did she stand in Blake's eyes against such loveliness?

Blake greeted her warmly, before drawing her towards Katherine.

'You remember Mistress Blair, don't you, Margaret?'

Her face lit up. 'Of course,' she smiled. 'Katherine and I met two years ago when I went to Ludgrove Hall with Rupert. I'm happy to meet you again, Katherine. Blake tells me that this is your first time at Court. Tell me, what do you think of it?'

'It's all so very exciting and new to me,' she replied, noting the peaceful quality to Lady Margaret's voice. 'It's so different from anything I've known and it will take a long time before I become properly acquainted with it all.'

'I know what you mean,' laughed Margaret, linking her arm possessively through Blake's.

'Are—are you to remain in London long, Lady Margaret?'

'Possibly two weeks—no more,' and she favoured Blake with a conspiratorial smile. 'I'm returning to Oxfordshire to make arrangements for our wedding,' she murmured softly. 'Has Blake told you that we have decided it will take place next month?'

Katherine felt her heart leap with dismay as Blake caught her eye, but quickly averted her gaze— she could not trust herself to look at him. The expression on her face did not change. After all, it had to happen in due course. It was what she'd both dreaded and expected. It was hard, but she must smile and let no one know how wretched she felt.

'So soon?'

'Yes. We have waited over a year and Blake has been absent for such a long time that we see neither sense nor reason in delaying any longer.'

Blake was looking at Katherine intently, as if to assess the effect Margaret's disclosure would have on her. He had wanted to tell her himself but somehow hadn't found the right moment. Amelia knew but had obviously said nothing to Katherine. Although, he thought, why should it matter to him what Mistress Blair thought? But he could not escape the irritating fact that it did.

'Then I wish you both every happiness,' said Katherine graciously, feeling the tears sting her eyes. She swallowed down a hard lump of disappointment and misery that had risen in her throat. 'Truly.'

'Thank you, my dear,' smiled Margaret, reaching out and squeezing her hand, 'but I have to say that, looking as lovely as you do, it won't be long before some fine gentleman captures your heart.'

'Which reminds me,' said Blake, 'there is someone who is eager to be introduced. Come, Mistress Blair. I think I see him now.'

Blake guided Katherine to where a group of courtiers were merrily conversing with each other, and he seemed to single one out with particular care which made her inclined to think he had something up his sleeve and set off a feeling of alarm.

The young man he introduced to her as Lord Soames was of boyish, personable appearance, slender, with light brown hair and rather soulful brown eyes, but it didn't take long for Katherine to realise that Blake had contrived this meeting, that Lord Soames was more than likely the first of the gentlemen he intended to parade before her, whom he considered suitable for her to marry.

Dismay washed over her and pain twisted her heart. Would she never learn? There was little wonder he had been so attentive, so keen to accompany her to Whitehall, when all the time he had every intention of abiding by his promise to her aunt to find her a husband.

Katherine would not give Blake the satisfaction of letting him see how hurt she was. Swiftly her eyes sought his. He saw the softness had gone from her face—she looked alert and challenging. He smiled, telling her that Lord Soames was from Devon, but his smile maddened her, whipping up her anger. Her eyes flamed rebelliously and her chin went up stubbornly. Forcing herself to remain calm, she turned away from him, leaving him in no doubt as to the depth of her anger.

Focusing all her attention on Lord Soames, she bestowed on him her most radiant smile. Hearing the music start up, she placed her hand on his arm and allowed him to lead her away from Blake towards the dancers who were congregating across the room.

*   *   *

For the rest of the evening, which had lost some of its magic and which Katherine now wanted to end, she could not prevent her eyes from straying to Blake but, since he talked intimately with Lady Margaret, he had plainly ceased to notice she existed. No one looking at her would guess, as she laughed and tossed her head at one of Lord Soames's compliments, at the depth of misery in her heart.

To everyone present she was outstandingly beautiful—undoubtedly the most beautiful woman in the room and the centre of attention. As the crowd of admiring young bloods thickened around her, complimenting her outrageously, vying with each other to dance with her, Katherine could not fail to be aware of her growing popularity and looked to see if Blake was aware of it also. With immense satisfaction she saw he was, for he was scowling angrily.

Fluttering her fan vigorously, she turned from him and in defiance made it look as if she were enjoying herself, throwing herself into the lively dance, smiling invitingly at the young buck intent on flirting with her, setting out to provoke Blake—a game she overplayed. He recognised it immediately and her deliberate attempt to draw attention to herself brought about his deep displeasure.

Lord Soames was utterly captivated by Katherine, his dark liquid eyes swimming with the same kind of adoration that reminded her of a small liver and white spaniel she'd once had as a child. Continuing to draw attention to herself, she laughed too loud, conversed too long, totally ignoring Blake—although she could feel his dark eyes burning holes into her back. Fury at his arrogant assumption that he could light-heartedly select a husband for her at will, without consulting her first on the matter of choice, was too much to be borne.

Finally, unable to watch her making a fool of herself any longer, Blake decided that it was time to leave.

It was then that Katherine felt someone's fingers grip her arm. Turning, she saw Blake. Not a feature stirred on his face but she could sense his anger.

'Come, Mistress Blair,' he said very calmly. 'The hour is late. It is time to leave. I am sure these gentlemen will understand if I whisk you away.'

They didn't understand and stared at Lord Russell incredulously. Ignoring their protestation she drew Katherine away, unable to stop her as she turned her head and smiled gaily back at their disconsolate faces. After bidding the King and Queen goodnight they left the gathering. The Earl of Rockley and Lady Margaret were not yet ready to leave.

Walking along the Stone Gallery to return to their carriage which was waiting for them in the Palace yard, they saw none other than the debonair, elegantly attired rake, Lord Forbes, moving towards them. As he recognised them, surprise registered on his face, which then broke into a charming smile, and he stepped aside to let them pass, making

Katherine an elaborate bow as his eyes swept over her with confidence and familiarity.

To drive Blake to even further anger, Katherine favoured Lord Forbes with her most ravishing, appealing smile as she passed by. When they finally reached their carriage, Blake's face was as black as thunder.

CHAPTER SEVEN

BLAKE was silent all the way back to Landale House, as was Amelia, for the threatening quality of his behaviour and the stern mask of his face, that she knew in all its moods, had rendered her silent. She suspected by his black look that something was gravely amiss, that once again Katherine had succeeded in antagonising him. How Amelia wished she wouldn't provoke him to such fury.

Katherine sat opposite Blake where he lounged in the corner of the carriage, looking frighteningly angry, the marble severity of his face etched sharply in the silver light shining in from the carriage lamps. She swallowed hard, a feeling of fear steeling through her. No doubt she would experience the full force of his fury when they arrived at Landale House.

Katherine was right; the minute they entered the drawing room Blake turned his simmering anger on her. Amelia hovered in the doorway, wanting so much to retire to her room yet afraid of leaving Katherine alone, feeling very strongly that a battle was about to erupt.

Katherine faced Blake who stood watching her, his eyes as hard as granite, and suddenly he seemed taller and darker than usual.

'Well?' he demanded, tossing his gloves into a chair and moving to stand over her intimidatingly. 'I await your explanation. What have you to say for yourself—of your astounding conduct? It would appear that you had suddenly taken leave of your senses. Your behaviour was disgraceful. Your performance impressed no one.'

'I was not out to impress anyone, my lord. I was merely being polite and enjoying myself. What is so wrong with that, pray?'

'Then did you have to do so in quite so open and outrageous a manner? 'Tis clear you do not understand the virtue of restraint and 'tis small wonder Lord Soames did not run a mile.'

'Why—this is most interesting. It is important what Lord Soames thinks, is it?' she fumed and the smouldering, quarrelsome inner fire which possessed her came to the fore, lighting her eyes with anger. 'How dare you try to manipulate me in this way? Is it your intention that I cultivate his friendship in the hope that I shall marry him?'

Blake's eyes narrowed dangerously. 'Marriage? Did I once mention marriage?'

'Do you deny that you introduced me to him with the intention of arranging a match between us? Without any reference to my feelings?'

'Why not? He is a good, honourable man and comes from a respectable, well-to-do family. I do not deny that I consider him a good prospect for a husband. After all—that is your reason for being here in London,' he said icily. 'I had assumed you understood that by now.'

'You seem to have a curious urge to make decisions for me, my lord, as if you alone possess the key to my future happiness.' She sighed deeply, lowering her eyes, suddenly feeling chilled to the heart, wanting nothing more than to cast herself into his arms, but since Lady Margaret had told her of their impending marriage her pride forbade her to yield to his desire that she wed another. Miserably unhappy, she had no choice but to stand firm on this.

'I told you that when I marry it will be to a man of my own choosing—not yours.' She spoke simply, without anger, merely stating a fact which Blake had to contradict.

'That is unfortunate—although, with a look like that,' he said, referring to her brooding countenance, 'you will frighten away any eligible suitor.'

'Then, if that be the case, I shall have to retain this look,' she quipped, looking more unhappy than ever and turning down her mouth at the corners. 'You cannot force me to marry anyone.'

'Can I not?' Blake hissed through clenched teeth. 'If needs be, I will. You have no choice. At the altar you will speak your words as instructed.' But even as he spoke he knew it was going to be no simple matter to marry off his stepmother's ward.

'No. I am not a chattel to be disposed of at your will. You are a brute, my lord, cold, cruel and heartless, for only someone with a black heart would treat a person so abominably.'

'Your opinion of me is of little interest, Mistress Blair,' he said, his eyes fierce, his voice like thunder, 'and I'm beginning to feel some sympathy for your aunt. It cannot have been an easy matter dealing with your disobedience all these years—whereas I will not abide your insolence. The sooner you are wed the better. Mayhap a husband will curb that viper's tongue you unfortunately possess and your wilfulness. And while we are about it there is the matter of Lord Forbes.'

'Oh?' Katherine had wondered how long it would take him to come to that.

'Your attitude towards him, your look, which has far too much eloquence, encourages him. It amazes me that a woman with your intelligence can tolerate such a fool. No doubt you will see him again about the Court. You will ignore him, of course. The man is a scoundrel.'

'An affable and charming scoundrel, you must admit,' said Katherine with an infuriating, barely discernible quirk to her lips, which Blake could not but fail to see and goaded him to further anger.

'Nevertheless, you will ignore him.'

'No. I protest. Why should I?'

Blake thrust his face close to hers, his eyes glittering like two black coals. 'Methinks you protest too loudly and too often, Mistress Blair. You will do as I say. I will not have your name coupled with the likes of him. There are many at Court with reputations of ill repute. You will steer clear of them. Do you understand?'

'By all accounts in the past you were equally as promiscuous—whereas now you behave like a reformed rake,' snapped Katherine accusingly.

Her words caused Blake to draw back apace and regard her steadily. His anger abated, somewhat, and he nodded slowly. 'Aye—maybe you are right. But at least I have the good sense to see the error of my ways.'

He turned from her, suddenly weary of this conflict that existed between them. Since Margaret's disclosure of their wedding arrangments there was so much he wanted to say to her, but he only succeeded in drawing out a long and painful silence. He sighed deeply.

'Must you be so disagreeable all the time?' he said, turning once again to face her, his face lined with strain. 'Your behaviour this evening was quite outrageous, you must admit. I possess a greater power over your senses than you give me credit for and I realise it was a show you staged for my benefit—to infuriate me for introducing you to Lord Soames without prior warning. Well—content yourself in knowing you succeeded.'

Surprised at the unexpected change in Blake's tone, Katherine took a deep breath. His eyes were as soft now as a moment before they had blazed with anger. She had been bitterly furious at his lack of consideration, of introducing her to Lord Soames without first consulting her, but he was right, there had been no need for her to behave so outrageously—and, moreover, she was honest enough to admit her wrongs.

'You are right,' she said softly. 'I do ask your pardon. I behaved badly. But I was so angry when you introduced me to Lord Soames. I knew what you intended. Only why did you not tell me? Why did you not prepare me?'

'I realise now that I should have.'

Taking advantage of the softening of his mood Katherine came to stand close to him. 'Why must I marry? Why can't things be like they were when I was at Ludgrove Hall? Why?'

At the sudden note of anguish in her voice, for an instant Blake leaned towards her and looked as if he were about to reach out and put his hands on her shoulders. She even moved closer towards the expected gesture of affection. But Blake stopped himself, thinking of Margaret, and stiffened, trying to check his own emotions as well as hers; because of this he unwittingly made his words sound harsh and peremptory.

'You are no longer a child, that is why, and you cannot remain at Ludgrove Hall indefinitely.' In truth, Blake would not be able to endure her closeness at Ludgrove Hall once he was married to Margaret. She would be even more of a threat to his peace of mind than she was at present.

Katherine stared at him. Drawing herself up straight, she sighed with resignation, having to admit defeat.

'You disappoint me. How quickly you forget what you said to me on the day at Ludgrove Hall when I asked you to speak to my aunt on my behalf—to allow me to leave for London with Amelia. I remember the occasion vividly.' She spoke softly and with meaning, her gaze holding his, forcing him to remember, also, what had transpired on that day— the kiss, which neither of them could forget.

'You told me that Ludgrove Hall was as much my home as it was Matilda's or Henry's for as long as I chose to make it so. How foolish of me to believe you meant it. But never fear, my lord. I shall marry if that is what you desire. Maybe if Lord Soames proves to be as satisfactory to me as you say he is, then it could very well be him—or someone of my own choosing. We shall see. But whoever I choose, I give you my word that I shall do so quickly—and so relieve you of all responsibility where I am concerned.'

Turning away, Katherine walked from him. Brushing past Amelia who still stood in the doorway, she left the room, beyond knowing or caring what she was to do next. Blake had driven her away. He had made it plain he wanted rid of her. Beyond that she could not think.

* * *

From where she stood in the doorway Amelia eyed her brother seriously, before moving slowly into the room, coming to stand before him. He looked quite wretched.

'Katherine is quite right you know, Blake. Since father agreed to her coming to live with us Ludgrove Hall has been as much her home as anyone's.' Her brother glowered at her from beneath his lowered lids, causing Amelia to sigh. 'Oh, dear. How she does antagonise you.'

'Aye. The wench has some growing up to do,' he growled.

'If you did not quarrel every time you meet, you might see her for what she is. From what I have seen of her since her arrival in London—and every other male at Court today could see—Katherine has come of age. She was undoubtedly the most beautiful woman there. She is no longer a child, Blake.'

'Do you think I don't know that?' he flared. 'Do you think I haven't seen the way others look at her? Oh, yes, she's beautiful—no face more lovely or form so perfect—but she is not for me, Amelia.'

'Come, now,' said his sister gently, 'I am not blind. I have seen the way your eyes seek her out in company. Why, at Court you were positively incensed by the attention being paid to her. Anyone can see you're more than fond of her. Are you quite sure you're not in love with her?'

'Don't be ridiculous,' he retorted fiercely. 'It is Margaret I love, Amelia, Margaret I will marry.

Mistress Blair is too impressionable, too difficult for her own good and as obstinate and stubborn as a thousand mules—with the temper of a savage and the tongue of a wasp. Any man who marries her will be welcome to her.'

Amelia suppressed a smile. 'Oh, dear. I do believe you have just given me a perfect description of yourself. You are too hard on her, Blake. It has not been easy for Katherine, living at Ludgrove Hall. Her aunt has always been against her and of late— well—I feel there is something troubling her. I know it.'

Blake glanced at her sharply. 'What makes you think that?'

'I'm not sure—but there is something. Perhaps if you weren't so busy at the docks all the time—and trying so hard to find her a husband, you would see it, also,' she reproached. 'Maybe she is all these things you say, but she does mean well and has the softest heart. I have watched her, Blake. I have seen the look in her eyes whenever they alight on you. She loves you—that is plain—and I believe she has done so ever since she first came to live with us at Ludgrove Hall.'

Blake looked at her as if she had taken leave of her senses. 'Nay—that is impossible. 'Tis imagination—infatuation—call it what you will, Amelia— but love?'

'Yes, I believe so.'

'Then that is unfortunate for Mistress Blair.'

'Nevertheless, do try to be more patient with her, less hard on her.'

'I will try, but if only she will endeavour to be less antagonistic towards me. Every time we meet she brings out the worst in my nature.'

Amelia sighed. 'If you are in love with her, then you must do something about it, Blake, for there will come a day when you can no longer struggle against it and it is Margaret who will be hurt. I know that love is rarely a matter for consideration in most upper-class marriages—but it is because there are so many cold marriages that men and women seek their pleasures elsewhere.'

Blake looked down at his sister, seeing a deep inner sadness in her eyes. Her own marriage to the Earl of Landale had come as a huge disappointment to her. What it lacked in passion she made up for in other ways, but no amount of laughter and gossip, of extravagant socialising and a wide circle of friends, could make up for her loveless marriage.

'I shall marry Margaret,' he answered firmly. 'I would not betray her trust and I do love her. Perhaps not in the way I should—but I admire her. I love her gentleness, her purity. We have mutual respect and understanding. What more is there?'

Amelia moved closer and looked deep into his eyes. 'A great deal more, Blake. Although you will not admit it, you know it yourself. I have not seen the same intensity of feeling between you and Margaret that exists between you and Katherine.'

'Enough,' said Blake fiercely, suddenly angry, for Amelia had touched on a raw nerve. For his own self-protection he purposely didn't want to think of Katherine, of her courage, her spirit, her fire, which he could not help but admire and which, although he would not admit it, appealed to his primitive soul. 'Margaret and I will be married—as will Mistress Blair as soon as it can be arranged.'

'And if you think you will be free of her then— when she is out of sight and married to another— then you are a fool, Blake.'

He nodded. 'Maybe you're right. I don't know. But I have lived by the code of honour I learned at our father's knee. I have pledged myself to Margaret. Nothing will make me break that trust.'

Amelia longed to plead Katherine's cause but Blake refused to listen and she could not pierce through the armour he had built around himself. But she knew her brother too well—nothing on earth would make him go back on his word to Margaret. It was Katherine she felt sorry for. Maybe Blake was right—the sooner she was wed the better it would be. She was young, young enough to get over her love and find someone else.

Amelia told her when they met the following morning, after Katherine came to her rooms complaining of Blake being a tyrant, 'Have a little more patience, Katherine, and do try not to antagonise Blake so.'

Katherine gave her a smile of affection. 'I don't

mean to,' she said, listening to the light-hearted laughter and banter of Amelia's ladies as they assisted her with her toilet, a function which never ceased to fascinate Katherine who, with the sole help of her own maid, Rose, had managed to do almost everything for herself all her life—and in a fraction of the time. 'Blake is always so disagreeable. Whenever we meet he rouses me to anger and my thoughts become muddled.'

Noticing how downcast Katherine looked, Amelia brushed aside the maid who was about to slip her dress over her carefully arranged hair and came and sat beside her. Her eyes seemed to bore into Katherine's innermost heart.

'Then perhaps it's because you are in love with him,' she said gently. 'That's it, isn't it, Katherine?'

Katherine stared at her. 'How did you know?'

'Oh—it's not difficult,' she smiled. 'Your eyes, your every look when you are together, betray you.'

Katherine nodded, swallowing hard. There was no use denying it. 'Yes. Oh, Amelia, there is nothing I can do—and yet I would do anything to win his love. There are moments when I think he cares for me—in a look—in a glance—but it means nothing. I do see that. I am right, aren't I? He's your brother—you know him better than anyone. He doesn't feel anything for me, does he?'

Amelia lowered her eyes lest Katherine read in them the truth, for she could not disclose any of the conversation she'd had with Blake the previous evening. That would be disloyal.

'I am so very sorry,' she answered in a low voice, 'but what do you expect me to say? Oh, my dear Katherine,' she said with deep concern, seeing the sadness in her eyes, 'do not delude yourself with that hope any longer. Blake will marry Margaret and so I urge you not to resist his will. Find someone else to give your affection to. You will only succeed in hurting yourself if you continue to think of Blake.'

'What—more than I already have?' Katherine retorted bitterly.

'Yes.'

'What you are asking me to do is impossible, Amelia. You cannot stop loving someone just like that.'

Katherine bowed her head, feeling a deep sadness. In the time between her conversation with Blake the previous evening and now, she'd had plenty of time to consider the course she would take with her life. Looking up, she met Amelia's eyes and it seemed to her that she saw pity in them—which was one thing she could not endure. To hide her true feelings she forced herself to smile.

'Don't worry, Amelia, I'm not going to make a fool of myself over him or anything like that. I do have my pride and self-respect. I like Lady Margaret tremendously and would not wish to hurt her for the world. But I cannot help being jealous of her—which makes me deeply ashamed. That is why I must go. I cannot bear the thought of staying and seeing them together. That would be too painful. I realise now that my presence causes Blake some embarrassment so I will take my leave just as soon as the opportunity arises. When I have found myself a husband.'

Talk of marriage suddenly made her think of the young priest she had seen at Court the previous day, reminding her that there was something else she wanted to speak to Amelia about.

'Amelia—do you remember that day in Appleby when we were out riding and my horse lost a shoe?'

'Why, yes,' she replied, relieved by the change of subject. 'We took refreshment at The Black Boar.'

'Do you remember the young man who was also sitting outside while we waited for Thomas to get the shoe fixed at the blacksmith's?'

Amelia became thoughtful. 'Only vaguely. I didn't pay much attention to him, I'm afraid. Although... from what I recollect,' she smiled, 'he seemed to be more interested in gazing at you—when his head wasn't buried in his book, that is. Why?'

'Oh—it's just that I saw a priest at Court yesterday and I'm almost certain they're one and the same.'

Amelia frowned. 'But how can that be?'

'I don't know, but the more I think about it I become more certain.'

'You must mean Father Edmund. He was the only priest I saw yesterday. Owing to the recent increase in persecution against Roman Catholics, especially priests, they have either gone to ground or fled the country.'

'Yes—that's what Blake told me.'

'You must be mistaken, Katherine. It must have been someone who looked like Father Edmund. And anyway—what on earth would he be doing in Appleby?'

'Mmm,' murmured Katherine thoughtfully. 'That's what puzzles me. Still—perhaps you're right and I am mistaken.'

After her presentation at Court Katherine was made aware of Lord Soames, seeing him on occasion, knowing that he searched her out, but she had become so absorbed in the excitements presented to her at the Queen's residence, Somerset House, and Whitehall, that she thought little of him.

On Amelia's advice Blake began spending less time at the wharves, keeping strict watch over Katherine, seeing to it that none of the dissolute characters who hung around the Court compromised her. He had also given much thought to his sister's concern about her and, on studying her, he had to agree that she was right. When Katherine thought she was unobserved there were times when a sadness would enter her eyes and she would become deeply preoccupied with her thoughts.

He thought back to the day at Ludgrove Hall when she had sought him out, almost begging him to allow her to go to London with Amelia. He remembered how upset and angry she had been when he had refused to speak to her aunt on her behalf, and he had suspected then that something unpleasant had passed between them, but he had thought little of it since. Whatever it was, could it still be troubling her?

With the intention of seeking a husband uppermost in her mind, Katherine relaxed into the general atmosphere and gaiety that surrounded the Queen, despite her aura of sadness caused by the recent troubles. On occasion she was acutely aware of Father Edmund, watching her from a distance, and she began to feel uneasy and disturbed by his regard. But, strangely, perhaps because he was a priest, unlike other men, there were no danger signals emanating from him—nothing amorous or suggestive in any way.

Lord Soames, however, was a different matter. He was totally captivated by Katherine's beauty, seeking every opportunity to become better acquainted with her, but he became dismally confused by her indifference and the lengths she would go to to avoid him. After all, Lord Russell had expressed his desire that they become acquainted.

It was not that Katherine disliked him; she found him pleasant enough and charming to be with—but so were many other gentlemen who surrounded her, not only handsome young gallants of the Court but also a colourful gathering of poets and writers whose effusive compliments she accepted most graciously.

Seeing nothing improper in acknowledging Lord Forbes, Katherine often cast him a smile—more to add to Blake's irritation than anything else. Yet she was sadly too inexperienced in Courtly matters to realise that, as she indulged in her mild flirtation, her friendliness could be construed as something else by him, for Lord Forbes did take it seriously. Katherine Blair was a beauty and a prize he still meant to have—however strong and obstructive the opposition.

Father Edmund was present at a dinner they were invited to being given by Lucy Hay, the Countess of Carlisle, a beautiful widow and member of the Queen's bedchamber. Her lodgings were down Cockpit Lane, close to the recreation area of Whitehall Palace.

Katherine's eyes were drawn to the priest immediately. Regardless of Amelia's insistence that Father Edmund was not the same man they had seen in Appleby, Katherine was now convinced that it was.

Blake watched as her gaze kept wandering to the priest until his patience snapped. Having taken her to one side as they waited to be ushered into dinner, he was prompted to say, 'If the fellow weren't a priest I'd say he wanted to make an assignation with you.'

To which Katherine replied tartly, 'And if he weren't a priest then maybe I'd accept.'

Blake's eyes narrowed. 'So, you are attracted to him?'

Katherine stared at him. He was so close she could feel his warm breath on her cheek and she wanted to say—not in the way she was attracted to him. Father Edmund did not possess the same powerful male aura that drew her to Blake, nor did she experience the warm tide of feelings that overwhelmed her and made her want to fall into his arms, to feel his lips on hers. It wasn't like that, but how could she make Blake understand?

'No, of course not,' she sighed. 'Not in the sense you mean, anyhow. I told you—he seems familiar. I believe I have seen him before, that is all.'

Blake became curious. 'Can you remember where?'

'Yes. In Appleby.'

He seemed surprised. 'I cannot for the life of me imagine what Father Edmund would be doing in Appleby—unless he was on some private mission to a Catholic family there. An act he could have been hanged for if discovered.'

'But he was not wearing clerical garb that day.'

'Missionary priests disguise themselves in both name and apparel—and many in their behaviour, so that no one would think or suspect them of being priests or popish scholars. I don't doubt Father Edmund will be well practised in the art of such deception,' he said drily.

Katherine frowned up at him. 'You are unduly harsh whenever you speak of him.'

'Nay. I've told you I have nothing against him, but

the fellow does have an irritating habit of vanishing completely and then reappearing when you are present—skulking around in the shadows. I've a mind to have a word with him and see what he's about.'

Katherine placed a restraining hand on his arm as he was about to move away to where the priest was quietly conversing with a group of people across the room. 'No,' she begged. 'Please do not draw attention to the situation or myself. I'm sure you read too much into it.'

Blake turned and looked down into her upturned face, noticing how her skin glowed in the light from the numerous candles. Conquering a traitorous rush of tenderness he sighed, smiling softly. 'Aye—maybe you're right at that.'

Katherine moved on, hoping to divert his attention from Father Edmund. Of late, not once by a look or a word had Blake betrayed to her anything other than the affection of a guardian or a friend, but he had ceased to be disagreeable whenever they were together, keeping to the limits of punctilious courtesy. This saddened her far more than his harshness, so she was more than happy for this rare moment of conviviality between them.

'I am surprised Lady Margaret isn't here with you this evening,' she said as Blake fell into step beside her.

His face became troubled and his dark eyes

clouded. 'Margaret has already left London for Rockley Hall.'

'Oh,' said Katherine with some surprise. 'But I understood she wasn't to leave for several days yet.'

'She didn't intend to but she wasn't feeling well. Her father thought the country air would be beneficial to her recovery.'

'Dear me,' Katherine replied with some concern, for she had thought Lady Margaret looked unwell on their last meeting. ''Tis nothing serious, I hope?'

'I pray not. Although, according to her father, she has not enjoyed good health for quite some time—becoming tired after the least exertion.'

'Then ought you not to have gone to Oxfordshire with her?'

'I wanted to, but she wouldn't hear of it. The wedding arrangements have had to be postponed until she's feeling better—but I cannot deny that her health does give me cause for some concern and I feel that her father is more anxious than he admits. Margaret makes light of it, scarcely allowing her feelings to be alluded to.'

'Then I shall pray that the country air and rest will soon make her feel better.'

Blake smiled down into her wholly sympathetic eyes. 'I know she would appreciate your concern. I just wish she hadn't been so adamant that I remain in London, but then—' he laughed, his eyes losing their troubled look and dancing mischievously '—I still have a husband to find for you. I'd be failing in my duty if I did not abide by my promise to your aunt to do just that. And besides—you do need some protection with Lord Forbes prowling the corridors of Whitehall like some predatory animal.'

Katherine smiled. 'You need not worry yourself about Lord Forbes. I was foolish once, and in my foolishness allowed him to escort me to London—believing him to be a gentleman.'

'A gentleman would not have taken advantage of your foolishness—and I still do not trust the fellow.'

'Do not worry yourself on my account, my lord. I think your display of solicitude and concern for my well-being boils down to your perpetual desire to be rid of me.'

She spoke lightly, with a hint of mischief, which had always bewitched yet often angered Blake. His face took on a seriousness when he spoke and, resting his eyes on hers, there was something in his voice which made Katherine's heart quicken.

'You are sadly mistaken if you think that. It is important to me that you will be happy and safe. That you can be sure of. I am aware that there have been times when you have been unhappy at Ludgrove Hall, that your aunt has treated you harshly, and it bothered me a great deal when she became intent on sending you to London to find a husband.

'You needed someone to guide you, to protect you, for you were ignorant of the realities of Court life, unfamiliar with the disciplines this would enforce on you and ill equipped to deal with the reprobates who loiter about. I was happy I was able to be here—however severe and disagreeable I must have seemed at times.' Although, he thought, much of his severity had been feigned for his own protection.

Katherine smiled at him, happy to see the warm friendliness in his dark eyes, but how she wished there was something else, for his marriage to Lady Margaret would not erase her love for him. She laughed with a lightness.

'Aye, my lord, there are times when you can be excessively disagreeable—but I do forgive you. I pray that once Lady Margaret takes you in hand she manages to tame you. Oh, see,' she said, glancing across the room. 'There's Amelia with Lady Carlisle, beckoning to us. I think everyone is beginning to move into the dining-room.'

Blake's brow creased into a disagreeable frown on sighting Lady Carlisle, which did not escape Katherine's notice.

'You frown,' she said softly, placing her hand lightly on his proffered arm as he led her towards the crush of people milling around the dining-room doors. 'I have a distinct feeling that you are not overfond of our hostess—that you would prefer to be elsewhere this evening.'

'I would have refused the invitation had my sister not cajoled me into escorting you both. I cannot for the life of me think what Amelia sees in the woman,' he growled.

'She's very beautiful and, I'm told, extremely wealthy.'

'And meddlesome and manipulative. She's the Queen's closest friend but I believe she plays Her Majesty false.'

'Oh? Why so?'

'She has close associations with John Pym—his informant, would be the correct term to use, I think. Our hostess has a passion for power with a will to be at the hub of things and to influence them. It is my belief that Pym and his colleagues are on a propaganda campaign and are behind the riots with an aim to break down the prerogative of the Crown beyond any hope of recovery—and—as happened with Strafford—to remove all the King's loyal councellors. Let us pray the Queen does not confide in Lady Carlisle too much—for it could have dire consequences.'

CHAPTER EIGHT

IT WAS at the end of the evening at the Countess of Carlisle's supper party, when Katherine was standing alone near the doorway, thronged with departing guests all awaiting their carriages, that she dropped her fan. She bent to retrieve it but at the same moment so did someone else, who picked it up before her. It was Father Edmund. He held it out and must have noticed how perplexed and shy she suddenly looked for he smiled.

'You dropped your fan.'

'I—I thank you,' she stammered, surprised at finding herself so close to him at last, noticing how soft his voice sounded. She took the fan from him. 'That was careless of me.'

'Not at all. We all drop things at times.'

'Pardon me for asking but—but it *was* you I saw in Appleby, wasn't it?' she asked in a rush of words. 'When I saw you at Court it—it came to my mind that I knew you. Forgive me if I'm wrong—if I were mistaken.'

'No, you were not mistaken,' he admitted calmly. 'I'm surprised and flattered that you should remember the occasion. I was passing through on my way to London—and—' he said, becoming thoughtful, 'I was hoping to see someone there.'

'Then I hope you were not disappointed.'

'No,' he smiled, revealing his white and even teeth. 'I was not—in fact, I was pleasantly surprised.'

Katherine looked at him curiously but they were distracted by Amelia crossing the room to join them. Seeming reluctant to be seen speaking to Katherine, Father Edmund stepped back.

'I must go,' he said in low, measured tone, his expression becoming suddenly serious, 'but it is important that you and I talk.'

Katherine fixed him with a puzzled, suspicious stare. 'Talk? But I don't understand. What can you and I possibly have to talk about?'

'There isn't time to explain now,' he mumbled hurriedly. 'I will contact you.'

Katherine stared at him in consternation. She noticed how blue his eyes were, that his features seemed familiar somehow. His gaze had always been enquiring and curious and she wondered why. Suddenly and from somewhere far back, came her aunt's voice saying his name was 'Edward—or something like it.' She thought it strange that she should remember this just now, but as realisation dawned on her, of the shape her confused thoughts were beginning to take, she froze.

At first she didn't feel anything at all. Everyone around her disappeared into a haze leaving her insensate, her face drained of colour as she stared in disbelief at the man taking his leave of her. No, said a tentative message travelling up to her brain. It isn't possible. It cannot be. But as he turned from her and disappeared through the open doorway, where the blackness of the night wrapped itself around him like a shroud, she knew that this man was her half-brother. Why else would he have shown such interest in her?

On the way back to Landale House Katherine had been unusually quiet. If Blake or Amelia had been aware of a change in her, they had given no indication of this, probably thinking she had been tired. It had been a long evening, and the hot sultry weather had still prevailed.

But Blake's sharp eyes had told him that something had occurred to bring about this change in Katherine. He'd observed Father Edmund pick up her fan and exchange words with her. Perhaps it had been innocent—maybe he had also remembered seeing her in Appleby that day—but why had he this insidious, nagging suspicion that it was something more?

That night Katherine had been unable to sleep with all the questions she had wanted to ask Father Edmund spinning around inside her head.

For days afterwards her mind had been in a confused and bewildered state. She had been impatient to see him, to talk to him, but she had been disappointed for she had not seen him again for quite some time, which she had thought odd. Until Lady Carlisle's party he had seemed to make a habit of materialising out of the stonework, often encountering her along the way, be it a corridor at Whitehall or Somerset House, or when she had been walking in the Palace gardens with Amelia and her ladies. So what had happened?

As time passed and still she had not seen him, she had begun to suspect that he had gone into hiding because of the rising frenzy of hatred against Roman Catholics in London. On all sides there had been widespread conviction that the crisis facing the nation had been the work of a conspiracy of papists. With alarm Katherine had heard how priests had been arrested—two had been brought to trial, one being the attendant of the Venetian ambassador, and had been sentenced to be hanged, drawn and quartered; not long after that, two English priests from the household of the Portuguese ambassador had been arrested. Fortunately, they had been rescued, but these tales reaching Katherine had made her afraid for Father Edmund's safety.

Whenever she had thought of him being her half-brother, the stark realisation of what it would mean had overwhelmed her with emotion, making her realise that the days before she had known him had been comparative peace compared to this new kind of horror which had taken hold of her, for she felt he had been caught in a powerful, relentless machine from which he would be unable to free himself, one which would eventually destroy him.

She had become noticeably withdrawn and preoccupied with her thoughts, spending less time at Court, which had become dispersed anyway since the King had left for Scotland to attempt to win the Covenanters to his side.

The Queen had moved to Oatlands, their country estate, where she had continued to suffer the ongoing hatred directed against her, for it had been suspected that she had conspired to have French soldiers brought over to England to aid the King in Scotland, and had sent out appeals to the Catholics in England to contribute money for an army to be used against fellow Protestants.

Finding the prospect of looking for a husband tiresome after her recent suspicions about Father Edmund being her brother, Katherine had found the long wait to see him intolerable. If he were indeed her half-brother, then why had he not sought her out? He had told her he would contact her. Do not let it be too long, she had prayed, for she would never rest until she knew the truth.

Katherine was alone in her room—Amelia having gone to the Exchange to purchase some materials for some new gowns—when news came to make her temporarily put all thoughts of Father Edmund from her mind. Lady Margaret Tawney had taken a turn for the worse and her father had written, urging Blake to go to Rockley Hall at once. Rose had rushed upstairs to tell her this; in alarm, Katherine went in search of him, finding him in the hall donning his hat and cloak, about to depart, a tense, anxious look on his dark countenance.

Picking up her skirts, Katherine hurried over to him. 'Forgive me but I had to see you before you left. Oh, Blake, I'm sorry to hear that Lady Margaret is so ill. Please convey to her my good wishes and I shall pray for her recovery.'

Blake paused and looked at her intently, the very whiteness of her face expressing the shock this news about Margaret had had on her—and the fact that she had unthinkingly called him Blake confirmed this.

Ever since the evening at Lady Carlisle's she had not been herself, rarely leaving the house except to go riding in the park. She had become absorbed and brooding, often staring vacantly at some unseen object, maintaining a strange silence, whilst at other times she seemed nervous and restless and he perceived a struggle going on within her.

'Thank you,' he said gently. 'I'm sure with such heartfelt prayers she will get well.'

'And—and with you by her side to give her added strength and comfort.'

'Aye—let's hope so.' A frown creased his brow. 'Before I leave, tell me what is troubling you? You have not been yourself of late. There is something on your mind—I can tell.'

It was more of a statement than a question and Katherine's heart soared with the unbelievable comfort of hearing the warmth in his voice, his concern for her, despite his own troubles. It had that strange effect upon her that made her long to cling to him, to tell him of the fears and terrors haunting her where Father Edmund was concerned.

Oh, if only he wouldn't fly into a rage if she confided to him that she suspected Father Edmund—a Roman Catholic priest—of being her half-brother. But she could not. Lady Margaret was ill, probably dying, and now was not the time for any words to pass her lips other than those of sympathy and hope for her recovery.

'I am grateful for your concern—but it is nothing—truly. And, anyhow, you have enough to worry about at this time.'

How she wished she could find some words to comfort him, but they failed her—yet here, alone in the hallway, she felt a closeness between them that she had never felt before and suspected he felt it, also.

Katherine was correct in her assumption. He had thought much of her of late, pondering over the conversation he had had with Amelia on the night Katherine had been presented at Court, and his thoughts disturbed him deeply and angered him.

He could not deny that she roused emotions and feelings in him no other woman had before—not even Margaret. And yet this anguish and betrayal he felt, at a time when Margaret was waiting for him and could be so close to slipping into eternal dark-

ness, filled him with profanation and made him feel
even more wretched and contemptuous of himself.

But he could not resist reaching out and taking
Katherine's hand. At his touch her fingers trembled
beneath his and she felt it hard to meet his eyes. She
had not realised that his fingers could be so strong,
yet at the same time comforting.

'You will take care, won't you?' he said, knowing
his duty lay with Margaret and yet feeling reluctant
to leave Katherine. His gaze slipped slowly over her
pale upturned face, seeing the luminous tenderness
in her eyes. She looked so defenceless, so childlike
and pure that he felt a strange urge to protect her
from whatever it was that plainly troubled her.

Katherine swallowed hard, her eyes never waver-
ing from his intense gaze. 'You need not worry
yourself on that score, my lord. It is hardly a time
for festivities with the King in Scotland and the
Queen at Oatlands. I shall not stray far from Landale
House, only to ride in the park. I shall anxiously
await news of Lady Margaret.'

Blake's fingers tightened before he released her
hand. 'Thank you,' he said hoarsely, not trusting
himself to say more or to remain with her any longer.

Katherine watched him pull on his leather gloves
and she thought her heart would burst with love. She
looked at him mutely, her mouth tinder dry and her
heart written all over her face. Blake's eyes met
hers, tortured, imploring silence, but every line of

his face admitted that he understood the truth of what her eyes told him.

As the door closed beind him, in that moment Katherine knew the hopelessness of despair, that, while ever he was promised to Lady Margaret, what was in her heart must remain unspoken. But he had reached out and taken her hand. Had she misread the signals that he cared for her after all? Had it merely been comfort he needed for what he knew lay ahead of him at Rockley Hall? She refused to let herself think what would happen if Lady Margaret were to die, for however much she loved Blake she did not want him at the price of Lady Margaret's life.

But would she ever be cured of this ill fated love she felt for him? This longing to have him close—to be near him always? She had always thought love would be a beautiful and wondrous thing but instead it was pain and torture to her heart, a living flame which would not be satisfied until it had consumed her peace of mind.

Katherine had fallen into the habit of riding in the park early in the morning with a groom in attendance. She would have preferred to ride alone but this was absolutely forbidden. She held her grey spirited mare, groomed to perfection and fretting to be off, to an impatient trot before reaching the park where she spurred her on to a faster pace, the mare's coat gleaming silver in the early sun.

She rode silently, revelling in the soft rush of wind in her face, breathing deeply of the cool, scented morning air, thankful that the suffocating summer heat had gone at last. Her groom, knowing of her love of riding, rode behind at a respectful distance. Few people were abroad which was why Katherine always chose to ride at this hour.

Upon seeing a horse and rider coming towards her out of a thicket close by, as if he had been waiting for her, she slowed her mount to a trot, watching warily as he came closer. The rider was shrouded in a large enveloping cloak, his wide-brimmed hat pulled well down over his features so that she was unable to see who it was until he reined his horse in front of her. It was only then that she recognised the handsome lean face of Father Edmund.

Katherine stared at him with a fearful look, almost too overcome to analyse her feelings now that she was face to face with him at last, finding it incredible to believe that this tall handsome priest, whose features she now realised resembled her own, was her half-brother. Suddenly she was swamped with immense joy that they had found each other.

'You!' she gasped. 'I had not thought to see you here.'

Father Edmund glanced around him furtively to make quite sure they were unobserved, aware of the dangers for both of them should he be recognised and she be seen talking to him. Satisfied that no one was paying them any attention he smiled, dismounting quickly, but Katherine could see by the tight lines around his mouth and the worried look in his blue eyes that he must be under considerable strain.

'I hope you don't mind my seeking you out like this. I could have sent a note to Landale House asking you to come to my lodgings, but being a priest and owing to the secrecy I am forced to employ—which I am sure you will understand—I was afraid it might fall into the wrong hands or you might be followed. I am aware of your habit of riding in the park at this hour; I have been waiting for an opportune moment to attract your attention. It is my intention to escape to France as soon as the opportunity arises and it is safe for me to do so, but I had to see you first. We must talk.'

Katherine nodded. Turning to her groom—who had just caught up with her, alarmed as to the identity of this person who had waylaid his mistress, was about to question him—Katherine instructed him to wait for her, dismounting hurriedly and insisting that there was no cause for concern because the gentleman was a good friend of hers. The groom held his tongue; he had recognised the priest and was confident that she would come to no harm.

Katherine fell into step beside Father Edmund; only when they were within the confines of the trees, partly hidden by their shaggy leafy branches, did they stop and face each other. To anyone observing them, their meeting could be construed as an early morning tryst between two lovers—which to them was just as endearing, for as brother's and sister's eyes met, devouring each other, it was as if to make up for all the lost years of their lives they had been apart.

Timidly taking both her hands in his, Father Edmund looked down at Katherine intently. 'You know who I am, don't you, Katherine?'

Swallowing hard she nodded. 'Yes. I—I guessed the truth at Lady Carlisle's party.'

'I thought so. I saw recognition in your eyes as I was leaving.'

'It wasn't just seeing you in Appleby that day. You were a stranger—and yet I felt that I knew you.'

'Many times I have been on the point of making myself known to you but I hesitated, afraid of the effect it would have on you. I have always known I had a sister—a half-sister—whereas you—I did not know what you had been told—that is, if you had been told anything about me at all. I had to admit that to confront you, to tell you who I was, could be a shattering experience for you. What do you know of our mother, Katherine?'

'Very little. Only that my father—when he insisted upon you and I being raised in the Protestant faith, which was against her own wishes as a Roman Catholic—learned that you were not his son and from that day on shut her and you out of his life. I was only a baby so I remember nothing. It must have hurt her dreadfully having to leave like that.'

'Yes. She never got over it. She devoted the rest

of her life to me—or what was left of it. She died when I was twelve years old, leaving me in the care of Jesuits in France. It broke her heart when she had to leave you behind—this I know. She talked about you often. I grew up knowing I had a half-sister. I was curious about you. I wanted to see you—to know what had become of you—what you were like.'

'What was she like—our mother?'

He smiled, a softening entering his eyes as he prepared to answer her question. 'You are very much like her. In spite of her folly she was a loving person, gracious and devout, which was why she took me to France to be raised within the church.'

'Why did you become a priest?' asked Katherine, curious about this brother of hers.

He smiled. 'I never considered doing anything other than entering the priesthood. I became a priest so that I could dedicate myself to God. I am bound to him as surely as any husband and wife are bound. I was ordained in Rome and it was there that I met Count Rossetti, a Florentine nobleman. When I learned he was to come to England as a private envoy to Queen Henrietta Maria, I came with him in the hope of seeing you—in spite of the open hostility directed against Catholics here. It wasn't difficult to discover where you were living.'

'I did not even know of your existence until recently.'

'How did you find out?'

'My aunt Harriet told me. She is my father's sister.

I was made her ward on his death when I was ten years old and taken to live at Ludgrove Hall with the Russell family.'

'I believe Lord Russell is away just now?'

'Yes. Lady Margaret Tawney, his betrothed, is extremely ill. He's gone to her home in Oxfordshire to be with her.'

Her brother nodded, having noticed how her eyes clouded over when she told him this. He had seen the way her eyes dwelt on Lord Russell, how they followed him, and he suspected that her feelings for him went deeper than she would care to divulge. 'And you? Do you like London?'

'Perhaps I would like it more if my aunt hadn't sent me here with the intention that I find a husband.'

He smiled. 'Oh? And have you?'

'No. There are several whom Lord Russell considers suitable but none I would care to live with for the rest of my life.'

'And what of Lord Forbes?' he asked tentatively.

Katherine looked at him quickly, thinking it strange that he should refer to him. 'Dear me, no. Lord Russell has a fit every time I look at him.'

'Small wonder. Lord Forbes is a man of notorious conduct—although,' he said looking at her meaningfully, 'I don't think you need me to tell you that.'

Katherine flushed hotly, embarrassed to discover that he obviously knew all about her indiscretion with Lord Forbes. 'Oh—you know about that?'

'Indeed, I do. As did most of the Court at the time.'

'Lord Forbes took advantage of my helplessness at a time when I needed a friend.'

'Please,' laughed Father Edmund lightly, 'do not feel you have to explain yourself to me. I know what happened and also the character of Lord Forbes. But I feel I must warn you, Katherine,' he said on a more serious note, 'to have a care. He watches you constantly. I fear that now you are no longer under Lord Russell's protection—in his absence—he will try and take advantage of you. I believe he is biding his time, waiting for an opportunity to get you alone so that he can compromise you again.'

Katherine looked at him in alarm. 'No—surely not.'

'I do believe so.'

Katherine smiled at him, feeling it strange and comforting that he should be so concerned for her wellbeing. 'Whilst I have been foolishly friendly enough, towards Lord Forbes, I am careful to be nothing more. Please—do not worry on my account.'

'Nevertheless, I cannot help but feel brotherly concern. Will you tell anyone that I am your brother?'

She shook her head sadly. 'No. At least, not yet. It is something I must get used to myself first. Besides—everyone will ask interminable questions and I do not feel able to answer them.'

'Yes, you are right.'

'And you? Will you admit that I am your sister?'

His eyes filled with loving emotion. 'I would like to tell the whole world but I fear that to do so would most likely condemn you. No one would believe that, being my sister, you are not a Catholic, also.'

'But what of you?' she asked, a look of earnest concentration on her lovely face as she suddenly became fearful for his safety. 'When I did not see you I thought something dreadful must have happened. I hear such awful tales about Catholics and priests being arrested—some condemned to death, even.'

Her brother's features hardened. 'Yes. That is so.'

'If only you had left England with Count Rossetti—for the very fact that you stood so high in his favour, and the Queen's, will lay you open to suspicion and the utmost danger.'

'Unlike Count Rossetti, I was not accorded the refuge of the Venetian embassy—nor was I allowed to leave the country with him. Count Rossetti is Italian whereas I am an Englishman so I was not granted any such concessions. Mr Pym may have agreed to his departure but an order was put out for my arrest.'

Katherine had gone very pale and her heart tightened painfully. 'But you may be caught.'

'I know—and there are those who search for me. I have taken refuge in a safe house close to the docks until it is safe for me to cross over to France. I can only hope my pursuers believe I have already left England.'

'If you are caught the penalty is death,' she whispered, feeling tears stinging her eyes, unable to bear the thought of losing him to a horrible death so soon after they had found eath other.

'I know. But if I am captured I will not deny my faith—and if it comes, then I have steeled myself to die. But if it should become known that you are my sister—that very fact could implicate you, also.'

'Oh, let it, for I do not care,' she cried passionately and her heart swelled with a great wave of tenderness. 'You are my brother—I cannot just abandon you to your fate now that we have found each other. If there is anything I can do to assist your escape, then I shall not hesitate.'

'No. And if there were I would not ask it of you,' he said examining her sweet beseeching face, her brilliant eyes awash with unshed tears, with a kind of wonder, for there was something in her pose that reminded him so very much of their mother. 'But it does my heart good to hear you say it, Katherine.'

He sighed, touching her cheek gently with his fingers, unable to believe that she was with him at last, that they were speaking like this. 'You know, when I returned to London after seeing you in Appleby, I was considering leaving for France immediately, but on hearing of your own arrival at the Court, I could not leave until I had seen you once more.

'And now—even if I am captured—my decision to remain will have been well worth it. This will be my reward: that I shall not have to endure, through the long years to come, the regret of never having seen or spoken to you. And now you must go. We have talked long enough. Your groom will become suspicious if we keep him waiting much longer.'

Panic seized Katherine. 'But will I see you again? We cannot part like this.'

'If God wills it, we shall. Now go, Katherine,' he said, taking her in his arms and placing a tender kiss on her cheek, now damp with her tears, 'and my love goes with you.'

Unable to speak, Katherine did as he asked and mutely walked back to her groom. Mounting her horse, she returned to Landale House.

As Father Edmund rode away he was unaware of the narrowed, watchful eyes of Lord Forbes, who had also been observing Katherine's movements of late. He had witnessed the meeting between her and the Catholic priest with some surprise, recognising Father Edmund when he had removed his hat and exposed his golden hair before entering the confines of the trees. Smiling broadly, he had been unable to believe his good fortune. On observing their embrace and fond farewell, he had immediately reached his own conclusion and thought the worst.

Well, well, he thought, gloating over this astounding discovery, so that was the way of things. Maybe he could use this to his own advantage, for how would Mistress Blair like it if he were to expose her indiscretion with a Roman Catholic priest?

Without hesitation he spurred his horse on, intending to follow Father Edmund to his hiding place. A warrant had been issued for his arrest, making the priest a fugitive—for hadn't Parliament concluded that the only way to save the nation was to purge the country and the government of such men? It could be in the nation's best interests if he were caught—and his own, of course.

At Rockley Hall, Blake mourned the tragic death of Margaret, his betrothed. When he had first arrived, he had been unable to believe the change in her; her condition had worsened and he knew that she was dying. She ate and drank only minimally, just enough to sustain life in her frail body, and the consumptive cough which attacked her like so many knives seemed to go on and on until she could cough no more.

Now she was dead, and the shock of this to Blake's system was deep and profound. He tried to hold in the crippling pain of her loss, but he could not escape the searing guilt that swamped his thoughts of not having loved her enough.

In his wretchedness his thoughts turned to Katherine, of the intimate warmth of their last meeting in the hall of Landale House, and the comfort it gave him to think of this; but he dared not let her image form in his mind although, despite himself, it was traitorously forming already. It was sacrilege to think such thoughts, before Margaret's pure and gentle body was hardly cold in her lonely grave. In fear of being so soon unfaithful to her memory, after having remained for a few days to share in the grief of her family at Rockley Hall, he went on to Ludgrove Hall to give himself time to overcome his grief and torment before returning to London.

CHAPTER NINE

THE rain had kept Katherine indoors the previous day, but today was fine and, when she took her usual ride, the silver-grey quietness of early morning possessed the park. Brown, bronze and gold leaves, still shining with yesterday's rain, blazed bright, spinning gently down from the tops of ancient trees and carpeting the ground with autumn splendour. A faint mist lined the horizon to the north and there was a strange, eerie quietude to the park that morning, with few people about. Even the small sounds of birds and beast seemed more subdued than usual.

Occasionally she glimpsed the odd rabbit and the bushy red tail of a squirrel, nimbly running along the branches of the trees or scampering in the damp undergrowth in search of nuts; even the solitary deer in the distance caught her eye as, fearful of the hunters, it ran for cover as she approached. Eventually Katherine slowed her horse down to a walk, feeling euphoric, her cheeks aglow with vitality, realising that she had been galloping hard, forgetting all about her groom. Her thoughts had been centred on Blake, wondering how he was—and Lady Margaret, for they'd had no word from him at Landale House since he had left three weeks ago.

She leaned forward and patted the neck of her sweating mare, seeing white blobs of foam dripping from the corners of her mouth. Suddenly, thinking it strange that she could hear no following hoof beats, she turned to see how far behind she had left her groom, but he was nowhere in sight. She stared about her, having ridden further than usual. This part of the park was completely deserted apart from a carriage ahead of her. For several minutes she waited, watching for her groom to appear, until her vague fears became a certainty that something must have happened to him.

Katherine was completely alone. A breath of cold wind drifted past her and she shuddered, for it came in the nature of a warning that something was afoot. She looked ahead when she heard the rumbling of the carriage as it came closer to where she waited, but thought nothing strange or alarming about this at that moment. It was only when it drew alongside, and she could see that its occupants were two gentlemen, that she felt the urge to ride away.

But it was too late—what happened then happened very quickly. Someone leaped out of the carriage and wrested her from her horse, bundling her roughly inside the carriage where, in the struggle that ensued, something was forced between her lips. In her surprise, Katherine swallowed the bitter liquid that trickled into her mouth, aware of the creaking and the swaying of the carriage as it hurried on its way. She struggled to fend off the weird sensations which began to take over her mind and body almost at once, but her efforts became weak. As she descended down into blackness, the last sight that she remembered was a vague vision of Lord Forbes, a triumphant smile of satisfaction on his slack lips as he watched her from where he sat in the corner of the carriage.

Gradually, she felt a vague emergence from unconsciousness to a feeble sense of existence. Katherine lay with her eyes closed, darkness all around her, at first remembering nothing, but slowly, as her senses returned, she was conscious of a terrible weariness in her whole body. She tried to move her limbs, but they were so heavy she could only lay where she was. Even her eyelids had a heaviness about them. She lay in a state of semi-lethargy for a long time—how long she had no way of knowing, for time and place had no meaning.

After a long interval she became aware that someone was in a room with her—two people, a man and a woman, and they were talking in low tones. Katherine made a positive effort to think, to remember, and tried to move her lips to speak, but no voice issued from her mouth. Someone was close to where she was lying and hands were placed beneath her head, raising it, placing something between her lips. A fiery liquid which she recognised as brandy was poured into her mouth which she swallowed, making her cough and choke, causing vigour to flow anew through her body.

At length her eyelids fluttered open and waves of nausea swept over her. She saw that she was not in her own bed, that this was not her room. The one she found herself in was larger than the one at Landale House, with an oriental strangeness to it, making her wonder if she had been spirited away to some foreign land. There was a sweet aroma, not unpleasant, of sandlewood and musk, and not even the candles' glow could diminish the vibrant, shimmering colours of gold and greens and blues of the embroidered wall hangings and jade and silver ornaments.

Heavy drapes hung at the windows, which were drawn so that she was unable to tell whether it was night or day. Katherine felt as if she were awaking from no ordinary sleep as the shadows in her mind began to retreat and shrink away. What was the strange potion she had been given to subdue her?

At last she looked fully at her captors. Recognising Lord Forbes, she realised that her tortures were to endure. Why hadn't she listened to her brother? He had warned her that this would happen, that Lord Forbes would take advantage of Blake's absence and seize the opportunity to compromise her again. She should never have gone riding in the park at such an early hour when few people were about. With some surprise she saw that the woman was Indian, tall and with jet black, glossy hair and almond-shaped eyes. She was dressed in a gold-spangled purple sari, with an assortment of delicate gold bangles circling her lower arms.

Seeing that Katherine was awake, Lord Forbes snapped his fingers and the woman scuttled out of the room, leaving Katherine completely at his mercy. Apprehension made her shrink against the pillows. As he moved closer to the bed where he stood looking down at her, she was revolted by him to the point where she was almost physically sick.

'Where am I? Why have you brought me here?' she asked. Her voice was almost a whisper, but she was surprised that she could speak at all.

'There is no reason to be afraid, Mistress Blair,' he replied, a sneer to his voice. 'I do not intend to hurt you.'

'No? Then what did you give me that rendered me insensate?'

'An opiate—quite harmless—but effective. A friend of mine, whose house this happens to be, is a merchant of the East India Company and travels extensively in the Far East. It is quite surprising the things he manages to purchase besides silks and exotic spices.'

Katherine closed her eyes, feeling so tired. Lord Forbes sighed. 'I had hoped you would come to me of your own free will but I began to realise that your smiles were false and meaningless. You were only playing a game with me, weren't you? Well—as it has turned out it was a dangerous game, one which, in your naïvety and innocence, you were unqualified to play.

'I like to play games, also,' he said smiling thinly, speaking slowly, 'but I never begin without an ace or two up my sleeve or a trump card. You see, I want more from you than you are prepared to give.'

Katherine opened her eyes and met his bold stare blazing down at her, insolently taking in her slender form beneath the silk covers and her frightened face. She was aware that she had been divested of her clothing and that a different, loose garment covered her nakedness. By whose hand she had been undressed she was too horrified to contemplate just then, but prayed it had been the Indian woman.

'You are speaking of my wealth, I believe?' she said coldly.

'And your delectable self, of course,' he said smoothly. 'Among the aristocracy wives are chiefly sought for their dowries and ability to provide heirs. Love has much more to do with mistresses. However, you, my dear, are fortunately well endowed with desirability and wealth. Put the two together and you have a perfect combination. What more could a man want in a wife?'

'What more, indeed?' replied Katherine scornfully. 'If you think for one moment that you will succeed with this insane plan, then you are mistaken. Think of the consequences of your action. My absence will have been noted by now and there will be people looking for me this very minute.' As she spoke her thoughts flew achingly to Blake, but he wasn't even in London so he would not have missed her.

'I don't doubt it, but they will not find you. No one will find you here. We are quite isolated. And—anyhow—I doubt Lord Russell will show much enthusiasm in searching for you. Rumour has it that his betrothed, Lady Margaret Tawney, has died and, grief-stricken, he has returned to Ludgrove Hall.'

Katherine stared at him in disbelief. No, that could not be true. Lady Margaret dead? Wretchedness swamped her; she knew how Blake must be suffering. Oh, if only she could go to him, to comfort him.

Lord Forbes smiled cruelly for it was plain by the shock in her eyes that she did not know this. 'So—you did not know of Lady Margaret's demise? Oh, well,' he sighed, ''twill make little difference to your situation. It would be much simpler if you comply with my wishes and agree to marry me. It would save everyone a great deal of time and trouble, you know.'

'You will hardly endear yourself to me by this show of violence,' she said through gritted teeth. 'Is it your intention to ravish me, Lord Forbes? To compromise me as before? For, as you see, you have rendered me quite helpless. It seems I am at your mercy.'

'Dear me, no. I said I never play games without an ace or two up my sleeve—or a trump card.'

'You talk in riddles, sir. Be done, if you please,

and speak plainly. I would rather die than marry you. Even if you keep me here for ever, I will never agree to that.'

Her captor smiled, his fleshy lips pulled back over his teeth, which reminded Katherine of a snarling animal. When he spoke his voice was as smooth as silk, but there was no disguising the underlying threat of his next words that made her blood run cold.

'No? What—not even to save the life of the priest?'

Katherine's heart missed a beat and her face went as white as the pillow on which she lay. 'Priest? What—what do you mean?'

Lord Forbes chuckled under his breath, pleased to see that his words had had their desired effect. 'Father Edmund. He is your lover, is he not? For why else would you meet him so clandestinely and at such an early hour in the park? Why, he is a fugitive—no less.'

Katherine stared at him in horror. 'He is not my lover. You blaspheme. He is a priest—a man of God.'

Lord Forbes raised his eyebrows derisively. 'He is also a man—who is equally as susceptible to the charms of a beautiful woman as the next man, priest or no. Deny it if you wish, but anyone observing the two of you that morning would take some convincing that you weren't lovers. Come—admit it, my dear. I saw you. Touching it was, too—and with such ardour. An affair of this sort would cause a merry scandal and no mistake if it came out.' He smiled, sensing victory could not be far away.

'Come now, use your common-sense. I shall put it plainly and leave you to think on it. Either you agree to marry me—at which I shall have the cleric brought here and the ceremony performed at once—or else I shall give Father Edmund up to the authorities. So— what is it to be?'

Overwhelmed by a terrible feeling of helplessness and despair, Katherine realised the terrible danger that could befall her brother. Lord Forbes would carry out his threat if she did not comply with his wishes, this she was sure of. She turned her head away so he would not see the tears start to her eyes. The man was a monster, cruel and unscrupulous.

'You cannot do that to force my hand. And anyway, how do I know if you are telling the truth? No one knows where Father Edmund is. He is in hiding.'

'From everyone else, I grant you, but not from me. You see, after I saw you together in the park I followed him. It is not the most comfortable of hiding places—close to the docks with the disgusting stench and rats—but a great deal more hospitable than Newgate.'

The mention of this infamous prison made Katherine blanch. Lord Forbes smiled coldly.

'Sooner or later you will agree to my terms—and if not—well,' he said, a low, threatening quality to his voice, 'the priest will be arrested and no doubt hanged and quartered—as is the practice—however unsavoury, but there it is. And you, my dear, well—people do have a habit of disappearing without trace.'

So, she thought, he would kill her also if necessary. Oh why had she not listened to Blake when he had warned her about Lord Forbes? What a stupid fool she had been, for she had brought this wretched situation upon herself. She had been thinking hard whilst she lay there, her eyes darting about the room, desperately wondering how she could escape from this prison, but Lord Forbes had guessed her thoughts and he laughed with gentle mockery, interrupting any thought she might have of escape.

'I will leave you to think about what I have said—but,' he said in menacing tones, 'do not forget that if you refuse me then the priest will die. And just in case you have an impulsive desire to escape I have taken additional precautions to prevent it.'

He clapped his hands once, the sound harsh and offensive to Katherine's sensitive ears, and at the command the woman returned.

'There is no way out of this room except by the door which will be guarded at all times. Sita,' he said, indicating the Indian woman, 'will also be with you for most of the time and should you prove difficult then she has orders to subdue you.'

That he referred to the opiate was plain to Katherine, causing a thrill of horror to shoot through her when she realised she might have to suffer another of his mysterious narcotic potions, which would plunge her into that terrible dark abyss where she had no control over her body or her senses. She shrank against the pillows in fear, shaking her head, the tears that she was too weak to repress flowing down her cheeks.

'No. You cannot.'

He smiled thinly. 'Yes, I can. You are completely helpless, Mistress Blair. I advise you to make up your mind quickly and then your ordeal will be at an end.'

Quite exhausted, the effects of the drug not having left her, again a wave of unconsciousness was sweeping over Katherine, making everything swim before her eyes. But before the drug-induced sleep took her over she glared at Lord Forbes.

'I hate you,' she whispered with great effort. 'I hate you.'

Lord Forbes gave her a twisted smile. 'I am not disturbed by what you think of me. I shall have you and your wealth. I am set on it.'

Katherine continued to lie in a strange apathy. She slept and woke intermittently. Sometimes the woman was in the room tending her. She spoke quietly, not unkindly, but when Katherine made an attempt to climb out of bed she was restrained by the woman, which took little effort on her part since all the strength had gone from Katherine.

She awoke during the night and, finding herself alone in the room with the light from just a single candle, managed to drag herself out of bed, but the effort of doing so made her head begin to spin and her knees to buckle. She fell in a heap onto the carpet. After several minutes she managed to draw herself up and crawl towards the door. Reaching up, she tried the handle but the door was locked. In despair and desperation she began to bang on it with all her might, but there was no one to hear.

Leaning against the door, exhausted, she looked around her prison. In a moment she took stock of her situation—alone in an isolated manor house, drugged and helpless in the hands of Lord Forbes who was biding his time until she would consent to marry him. He would have thought this through carefully, choosing the house where he would keep her prisoner with care, far away from anyone and beyond suspicion. She was alone in this house with her captors, unfrequented by anyone and the improbability of any help whatsoever. Oh, she saw it all and despair such as she had never known engulfed her.

Blake arrived back in London to find Landale House in turmoil. Katherine had been missing for four days now. It was as if she'd disappeared into thin air. Fortunately, the groom was none the worse for having been knocked from his horse by a sudden blow to the head from an unknown assailant, rendering him senseless for some considerable time. Amelia was beside herself with worry over Katherine's whereabouts, and deeply concerned about Blake and the grief he must be suffering on account of Margaret's death.

Blake was quite unaware that anything was amiss until he met Amelia in the drawing-room and saw the anxiety on her face. Initially, he thought it was purely out of concern for himself and nothing more.

Her two hands outstretched, she came to him quickly, seeing how weary he looked, with grief and strain etched on his dark countenance. How would he react when she told him of Katherine's disappearance?

'Oh, Blake—thank the dear Lord you're back. I was so sorry to hear of Margaret's death. So terribly sorry. It came as a terrible shock to us all.'

Blake looked at her calmly, his dark eyes heavy with fatigue. 'Yes—God rest her. At least her suffering is at an end.'

He frowned, suddenly aware that Amelia did not seem herself. She looked agitated and dark rings circled her eyes, making them look larger than ever. Her face was as white as the lace at her throat. He took hold of her hands, his heart already leaping with alarm in his chest, his senses telling him that something was badly wrong.

'Amelia, what's wrong?' he demanded. 'Tell me?'

Her composure finally broke. 'Oh, Blake—it's

Katherine. She's disappeared. No one knows where she is. We—we believe she has been abducted.'

Blake stared at his sister. His face whitened and horror and disbelief flared in his eyes. 'Oh—my God,' he whispered.

The words were barely audible but the horror in them shocked Amelia and she had no trouble imagining the thoughts going through his mind.

'How long has she been missing?'

'Four days.'

He stared at her, aghast. 'Dear Lord—she could be anywhere. Abducted, you say? Have you not heard anything as to her whereabouts? A ransom note? Anything?'

'No—no. There has been nothing. I know abduction by desperate lovers is not unheard of—and that where Katherine is concerned there are many eligible and titled men on the scene. But I cannot think of one of them who would be guilty of such a despicable act.' She began to cry with despair. 'What can we do? We must find her. Oh, Blake—you don't know what it's been like. Since her disappearance I have worried day and night. George is out this very minute looking for her.'

The sight of his sister's distress sent a pain through Blake's heart. 'Tell me exactly what happened?' he said gently.

'It was when she was out riding in Hyde Park. You know how she loved to ride in the early morning—when it was quiet and not many people were about?'

Blake nodded, swallowing hard. Yes, he knew. It was just like her, for it was a pleasure she had always enjoyed at Ludgrove Hall.

'Go on,' he urged.

'The—the groom who always went with her—aware how much she liked to give her horse its head when they reached the park—always rode at some considerable distance behind. On the day she disappeared someone—he did not see his assailant—knocked him from his horse. He was unconscious for quite some time and when he recovered Katherine was nowhere to be seen. Only her horse. It—it was as if she'd been spirited away into thin air,' she finished quietly.

'Did she ever meet anyone on her rides?'

'No, not that I know of. But—yes,' she said, suddenly thoughtful, 'there was just the one occasion when she was approached by a gentleman.'

Suddenly alert, Blake looked at her sharply. 'Oh?'

'The groom saw nothing unusual in this for she did seem pleased to see him. They both dismounted and walked and talked together for quite some time, it appears.'

Blake's expression became grim as he forced himself to ask the next question, strongly suspecting that the gentleman in question was none other than that reprobate Lord Forbes. 'Who was it? Did the groom know the gentleman?'

'Yes. It—it was Father Edmund.'

Blake stared at her incredulously. Amelia had taken him completely by surprise. 'Father Edmund?'

She nodded. 'Do you think he could have anything to do with her disappearance?'

He shook his head slowly. 'No. Whoever abducted Katherine resorted to violence. This I believe Father Edmund to be incapable of. Where is he? Does anyone know?'

'No. Some say he has left the country while others believe he is in hiding. A warrant has been issued for his arrest. Did you know this?'

Blake nodded. 'Aye. I expected it before now.'

'Like you, I do not believe he is capable of doing anything unpleasant. Besides—what would be his reason?'

'None that I can think of,' Blake replied. Although, he thought, Katherine's meeting with Father Edmund in the park was suspicious in itself. But it had to be coincidence—what other explanation could there be? Lord knows the man was handsome enough to cause many a feminine heart to flutter—and with the correct approach Blake was certain he would succeed in converting all the ladies who surrounded the Queen to Catholicism—but he was a priest and supposed to be far removed from all sinful pleasures of the flesh.

But he was not ignorant of the corruption and venality that besmirched some of these Catholic priests and the dignity of their apostolic office. His considered opinion was that these men were human, not divine, beings, who had spurned riches and earthly honours in order to promote piety and breathe a wholly heavenly spirit. And, he thought with cynicism, there were some he could think of who had oft broken their vows of chastity—but he doubted that Father Edmund could be numbered as one of them.

Blake remembered the evening at the Countess of Carlisle's when he had seen Father Edmund speaking to Katherine. However brief their conversation had been, he had been aware of her quiet preoccupation since then. He still discounted the idea that the priest had played any part in Katherine's abduction but he was baffled by the awareness they had shown in each other, nevertheless.

Unless, of courge, he hoped to make her a convert to his faith? But no, that could not be the reason. In fact, it was quite ridiculous, for to do so he must have a willing party and Katherine was not devout enough about religious matters. At least, she did not appear to be, but then, he thought, becoming troubled, how would he know? Had he not been away for most of her impressionable years of adolescence?

And then another thought occurred to him. Hadn't his father once told him that her mother had been a Roman Catholic? At the time he had thought little of it, his mind being full of other things, but if Katherine was aware of her mother's Catholicism, then perhaps her curiosity to know more had got the better of her.

But this did not explain her disappearance. It had to be someone else and there was only one other man he could think of who was capable of committing guch a dastardly act. Rowland Forbes. He had compromised her once, and when he recalled the way his eyes had followed her every movement since, he was wholly convinced that he was the man he should look for.

'Forbes,' he said suddenly. 'Lord Forbes. Now there is a man I believe is capable of anything to achieve his own ends.'

Amelia looked at him and nodded. 'Yes,' she said in a low and thoughtful voice, 'we thought of him, too. George has made enquiries as to his whereabouts but he has not been seen about London for ages. Besides—surely he would have demanded a ransom for her release by now?'

'Not necessarily. The lure that attracted Forbes to Katherine in the first place was her handsome fortune. She has enough money to enable him to live a life of absolute ease. But to abduct her forcibly against her will is monstrous. I doubt she went with him without a struggle. He will think that all he has to do is compromise her—as he tried to do before— and she will have no choice but to marry him.

'However, I believe he underestimates her. She has teeth and claws and would suffer the indignities of degradation and dishonour rather than surrender to his will. Send the groom to me, Amelia. I will interrogate him myself.'

This Blake did, but the man could tell him no more than he already knew. When he'd left the room, noticing the anxiety in her brother's eyes, Amelia placed her hand affectionately on his arm.

'Katherine will be all right, Blake. She's got to be.'

He looked down at his sister and their eyes locked in a silent prayer that she was right. But the thought of Katherine humiliated and bewildered in the hands of her abductor, especially if, as he strongly suspected, it was Lord Forbes, caused a dull rage to fill his being and, for an instant, everything seemed to go dark around him. He dared not let his mind dwell on the tortures she was probably being subjected to. But when he could think more calmly he remembered her loveliness, which had been overshadowed in the past by his devotion and betrothal to Margaret. Now he remembered with amusement and affection the times she had pitted herself against his will, and he realised that, however unpleasant her ordeal, Katherine had the strength and ability to survive until he could find her.

Following his instinct, fervently hoping that he was right to do so, Blake concentrated all his efforts on hunting down Lord Forbes and, hopefully, Katherine. He became like a man in the grip of a nightmare, refusing to rest in his determination to find her, but the task proved to be well nigh impossible—it seemed that Rowland Forbes had disappeared off the face of the earth. A trusted servant was sent to his home in Hereford in case he had turned up there, but the journey proved fruitless. Blake questioned everyone who knew him, exhausting all his usual disreputable haunts on both sides of the river, but still he came up with nothing.

News of Katherine's abduction went through the upper echelons of London society like gunshot, becoming all the gossip. Blake would have preferred to avoid this, but he had to admit that the more people talked of the affair the better chance he had of uncovering Lord Forbes's whereabouts—someone might remember something, however trivial, and come forward. And that was precisely what did happen.

It was late when the sealed note was delivered to Landale House. Blake was exhausted but still refused all forms of rest. His eyes were overbright, his skin stretched tight over his cheekbones, the strain of the past three days since his return to London evident, which left Amelia in no doubt as to the depth of his feeling for Katherine. Margaret's death had hit him hard but Katherine's disappearance had hit him harder, and she prayed that, for both their sakes, she was found quickly, alive and unharmed.

Amelia handed the note to Blake with shaking hands, watching with bated breath as he broke the seal and tore it open, scanning the neatly written words hungrily. Only when he'd come to the end did he look up, a slightly dazed expression on his face.

'What does it say?' asked his sister impatiently.

'That I am to go to the house of Sir Matthew Mayhew in Highgate.'

Amelia's brow puckered in a thoughtful frown. 'But—who is Sir Matthew Mayhew? I do not believe I can recall the name.'

'It appears that he's an acquaintance of Lord Forbes. He's a merchant with the East India Company who happens to be out of the country at present. It seems that he has temporarily let his house to Lord Forbes.'

Amelia permitted herself to smile with relief for the first time in a week. 'Oh, Blake—that's wonderful news. At least it's a lead which may take us to Katherine. Whereabouts in Highgate is this house?'

'It is called Wycliffe Manor—situated in an isolated spot close to the woods.'

'Who sent the note?' asked Amelia curiously. 'Does it say?'

Frowning, Blake glanced again at the note. 'No, that's what puzzles me. It's unsigned.'

'How strange.'

'Yes. Whoever it was must have good reason to wish to remain anonymous. Still—whoever is responsible I am grateful. It says I am to proceed with caution.' Folding the note he strode to the door with fresh impetus. 'There's no time to be lost, Amelia. I must begin making arrangements immediately.'

CHAPTER TEN

IN NO time at all Blake was riding towards Highgate, five miles north of the city of London. Many aristocratic members of London society, in order to escape the discomforts of the city, had taken to building themselves mansions on these pleasant northern heights.

Three capable men from the Earl of Landale's household rode with him, mounted on some of the Earl's finest hunters. Fortunately they were familiar with the countryside, but they were hampered by the rain which was lashing down out of heavy blankets of cloud, being driven across a moonless sky by a cutting wind, growing stronger with an ever-increasing force.

Such was Blake's determination to reach Highgate quickly that he completely disregarded the discomfort caused by the water collecting in the folds of his cloak and running in a thin stream down his neck. Hunched over their horses' necks they rode swiftly, concentrating all their efforts on their route, knowing where to take short-cuts down narrow lanes and over fields to lessen their journey.

On reaching the village of Highgate they quickly commandeered the services of two constables of the watch who, on hearing what they were about, led them to the home of Sir Matthew Mayhew.

Wycliffe Manor was a large Tudor manor house surrounded by a high wall. It stood gaunt and forbidding at the edge of a dense wood and, despite the raging storm, it seemed wrapped in utter stillness, its only sign of life being a dull reddish glow shining from the cracks in the heavy drapes covering the mullioned windows. The band of horsemen slowed their horses to a walk, advancing towards the house slowly and keeping to the grass so as to avoid any noise they would make on the gravel driveway leading up the the heavy doors of the house, and thus alerting anyone inside to their presence.

Beneath the shelter of some trees, which gave them brief respite from the still driving rain, Blake dismounted and indicated that the others should do likewise. His face was grim when he faced them.

'Remain close by my side and employ the utmost stealth. And remember—we have no idea what we shall encounter when we enter the house. Have your swords to hand but do not use them unless it is in defence of your life.'

With an awful sense of foreboding and dread in his heart at what he would find within the house looming before him like some giant animal about to uncoil from sleep, Blake moved towards it.

Meanwhile, having no idea that rescue was at hand, Katherine, having feigned sleep, had watched between half-closed lids as Sita, seated before the fire, had been lulled into a deep slumber by the warmth. After enduring a week of Lord Forbes's odious presence and his insistence that she would marry him in the end, Katherine had given him the false impression that she might be beginning to weaken. She had thought to hold out as long as possible in the hope of giving her brother time to leave the country, but she could see that Lord Forbes was becoming increasingly impatient and angry. It was imperative that she did something quickly.

Bent on escape, although she had no clothes other than the one shapeless garment which covered her nakedness, and losing no time, Katherine had watched and waited for an opportunity such as this— when Sita would fall asleep without locking the door. She slid out of bed and, after slipping her feet into a pair of slippers, moved stealthily towards the door. Her shaking fingers closed around the knob which she turned, pulling at it, drawing a deep breath of relief when the door opened soundlessly.

Peering out onto a long gallery, she discovered that there was no guard outside her room as Lord Forbes had indicated. Gingerly she stepped out, jumping nervously when she heard a door bang somewhere inside the great house. After a moment, and feeling confident that it was safe to do so, she moved along the dimly lit gallery, stealthily picking her way between pieces of furniture standing against the wall, moving towards a staircase ahead of her and soundlessly gliding down it to the hall below. Several passages led off from it, the candlelight casting deep shadows on the walls.

Hearing heavy footfalls moving in her direction down one of the passages, feeling utterly afraid, Katherine slipped inside a darkened room, pressing herself close to the wall while looking through a crack in the slightly open door. An elderly man, who she thought must be one of the servants, walked past, his footsteps heavy like the terrified beating of her heart. She remained where she was as she heard him move on down another of the passages.

Katherine was completely unaware of the figure of Lord Forbes standing stiffly by the window looking out, having been alerted by the faint sound of a horse whinnying over the noise of the storm. Ever since he had come to Wycliffe Manor he had been constantly on his guard. At first he had thought he had imagined the noise, for on a night such as this, with the driving rain thrashing mercilessly at the windows and falling faster and heavier by the minute, all sorts of noises were to be heard, but he soon realised he had not.

Peering out, he could just make out the dark shapes of men moving quickly across the grass towards the house, disappearing as they pressed themselves against the sheltering walls. Realising he must act swiftly if he was to prevent them entering the house, he turned from the window at the same moment that Katherine entered the room, and he realised immediately that she had somehow managed to slip past Sita.

Over the noise of the storm it was the sound of someone uttering an angry curse that impressed Katherine's sharply awakened senses, and she became transfixed by indescribable terror. Her knees began to shake when she realised that she was not alone in the room but, peer as hard as she might, she could make out nothing in the darkness.

She heard soft footsteps on the carpet coming towards her and she realised that whoever it was must have seen her in the shaft of light stealing in through the slightly open door. Some power that made flight impossible held her remorselessly there, her eyes glued to the place where she could hear the footfalls.

She uttered a shrill cry when she found herself suddenly seized and roughly picked up and swung over someone's shoulder. Only then, to her shattering dismay, did she see at a glance the grim features of Lord Forbes and she knew all was lost. Hurriedly he carried her back to her room where a worried-looking Sita had just realised that her charge had gone.

Placing Katherine unceremoniously on the bed, Lord Forbes issued an order, at which the Indian woman produced a small glass half-filled with liquid.

'You will drink this quickly,' ordered Lord Forbes.

Realising with a rush of horror his intent, that she was once again going to have to swallow the potent drug, which would render her helpless and plunge her into unconsciousness, Katherine gave an earth-shattering scream, desperately twisting and clawing at Lord Forbes as his cruel hands gripped her shoulders and pinned her to the pillows. The woman, with superhuman strength, stopped her head from thrashing about and forced the glass between her lips, pouring the bitter-tasting liquid into her mouth, her hand then covering her lips and nose so that she was unable to breath or spit it out, forcing her to swallow it down.

Katherine began to slip into unconsciousness as Lord Forbes picked her up and carried her towards the oak panelling, determined that no one would find her. At the same moment, alerted by Katherine's desperate cry, Blake abandoned all hope of trying to enter the house secretly and began beating with great urgency on the door.

It was the same elderly servant Katherine had seen earlier who opened the door to Blake. At the authoritative note in his voice the man stepped aside to let them pass, the newcomers dripping water from their sodden cloaks all over the floor. A few strides inside, Blake looked past the servant to another man coming slowly down the stairs.

So, thought Blake with grim satisfaction, I have found Forbes at last.

Looking surprisingly confident and self-assured, Lord Forbes was moving down the stairs calmly, considering Blake, a nonchalant, bored expression on his face, as if he'd been disturbed from sleep.

'Well, gentlemen,' he greeted them evenly, 'to what do I owe the pleasure of this unexpected visit? The hour is extremely late. I was about to go to bed.'

Blake's eyes narrowed. After the strain of the last few days he wanted to forcibly extract the information he required from this blackguard, but he had to admire the man's poise. He moved towards Lord Forbes menacingly, without taking his eyes from his, making a visible effort to control his temper.

'Don't take me for a fool a second time, Forbes,' he growled. 'You know perfectly well that we are here to recover Mistress Blair. Where is she? What have you done with her?'

Lord Forbes stared at him with absolute amazement. 'My dear fellow, I have really no idea what you are talking about—and why all these men?'

'We have reason to believe from this gentleman that Mistress Blair is in this house,' said one of the constables, stepping forward, beginning to wonder if he had been brought to Wycliffe Manor on a wild goose chase, but he had heard of the young lady's abduction. If he could secure her release, it would be a feather in his cap indeed. 'He strongly suspects that you have abducted her and are holding her against her will.'

Lord Forbes appeared in no way disconcerted by the accusation, and anyone would have sworn by his apparent concern for Mistress Blair that he was not a man so base as to go around abducting young ladies.

'Why—this is absurd. I have not seen Mistress Blair for some time—three weeks, I believe. If the lady has indeed been abducted, then I sincerely hope you find her. But why assume that it is I who took her?' he asked looking at Blake.

His surprise and anxiety seemed genuine enough to those who did not know of his unsavoury character, but Blake was not deceived.

'Knowing of your regretable passion for abducting young ladies—and that you are desperate to obtain a large amount of money to enable you to retain your property and pay off your innumerable debts—who else would I look for?' growled Blake.

Lord Forbes's eyes remained shuttered but Blake sensed his hostility, also a nervousness beneath the surface and some degree of agitation. Silently damning Rowland Forbes to hell and back, and unable to control his growing impatience, he thrust his face forward, his dark menacing eyes drawn together in a straight line as he glared at the man he would delight in beating to a bloody pulp for his dastardly treatment of Katherine.

'Before we entered this house we heard someone scream—a young lady, I would say. So—I will ask you again, Forbes, before we are compelled to search this house. Do you have Mistress Blair here?'

His voice was low and threatening, leaving Lord

Forbes in no doubt as to his hatred, and that, however strongly he continued to deny having any part in Mistress Blair's abduction, Blake was determined to seek her out.

He paled visibly. 'She is not here,' he said flatly. 'Now kindly leave this house and take your friends with you.'

'You lie, Forbes. Dealing with persons of your sort. . .one learns not to trust them. She is your prisoner—come—admit it? But I tell you this—if you have harmed her in any way then I swear I'll have your head,' Blake hissed. 'Now, where is she?'

At Lord Forbes's continued defiance all Blake's fears and anxieties over Katherine began to explode in his brain. In his anger he reached out and grasped Lord Forbes's cravat, pulling him close so that his face was on a level with his own.

'Aren't you forgetting something, you blackguard? I do not forget that you have tried this once before with Mistress Blair and that I still have a score to settle with you over that affair.' Blake released him suddenly, turning to those around him. 'Search the house,' he commanded. 'Enough time has been wasted.'

Lord Forbes stepped forward. 'I advise you not to. This is Sir Matthew Mayhew's house and he will not take kindly to you trampling through it. You'll be wasting your time, anyway. She is not here.'

'I believe she is,' said Blake with ominous coolness, 'and by the time I've finished with you, Forbes, you'll regret ever setting eyes on Mistress Blair.'

Like a tidal wave Blake and his men swept through the rooms of Wycliffe Manor, one by one, and to their surprise they met with no resistance for the house, built to accommodate a large staff, was unoccupied, apart from the elderly man and the strange Indian woman, who calmly watched them search the room Katherine had occupied until a little while before with little interest.

After a fruitless search one of the men, believing that Katherine was not there, suggested the scream they had heard could have been a trick of the wind, but Blake was adamant that it had been Katherine they had heard.

It was when he entered the room where she had been kept prisoner that he became convinced she was secreted away somewhere within the house. It was a strange house, filled with murals and mosaics depicting colourful Eastern scenes, with low divans strewn with velvet cushions, bordered with gold tassels and fringes, and rooms filled with exotic objects and curios, all accumulated by Sir Matthew Mayhew on his travels with the East India Company.

He noticed a strange lingering sickly sweet aroma which had invaded all the rooms of the house, mingling with musk and scents of Eastern essence. In one of the rooms he came across a curious collection of pipes, but took little notice of them just then, being intent on examining the walls, aware that this was a house built in Tudor times and that, as a precaution to secure the safety of priests, the construction of hiding places had been commonplace. A house such as Wycliffe Manor could have many such places.

He soon realised that the strange aroma was stronger in this room than in any other. On closer inspection of the pipes, he came across a small spirit lamp and a scale, the type apothecaries used for weighing powder for medicaments. He suddenly went cold at the suspicion beginning to form in his mind, for he knew that this was paraphernalia used by opium smokers—a drug he knew from his own experiences on his travels. It was derived from the opium poppy and grown in abundance in India, Turkey and China, where it had been acclaimed for its medicinal properties for centuries, but if misused it was known to corrupt and weaken the mind. Sir Matthew Mayhew would know all about it, for he had traded with peoples in the Far East for years. Lord Forbes was a close friend of Sir Matthew's, so it was possible that he could have obtained the drug through him.

Now Blake was truly afraid for Katherine's safety. Had Forbes drugged her to force her compliance? If so, her condition could be quite desperate.

He returned to the room where the Indian woman still hovered, her chiselled features unrevealing. She was obviously attached to Sir Matthew's household

for on investigation before he had left Landale
House for Highgate, he had discovered that Sir
Matthew Mayhew, who was well known for his
eccentricities, had a colourful array of foreign ser-
vants. Forbes had clearly engaged the services of this
Indian woman for the duration of his stay at Wycliffe
Manor.

Ignoring her presence, Blake became thoughtful,
gazing around, finding the room was much the same
as before, when suddenly his eyes became focused
on some lighted candles on a small table standing
close to one of the panelled walls.

He stared at them curiously, for he was sure he
saw the flames waver and flatten slightly, as if caught
by a sudden draught, though not strong enough to
extinguish them. But how could that be, he asked
himself, when there was neither window nor door in
the wall to cause a draught? At least not one that
was apparent.

With bated breath, hardly able to contain his
eagerness, Blake moved towards the wall and carefully ran his hands over the oak panelling, shouting
for the others to join him when he felt a faint rush
of cold air which indicated there was a cavity behind
it. Momentarily distracted by the swish of silk behind
him, he turned just in time to see the Indian woman
disappearing through the doorway.

Unperturbed by this, for he knew she wouldn't get
far, he again turned to examine the panelling, searching for something which could be a catch to open it.

Fumbling behind one of the wall hangings to his right at last his fingers came into contact with a small projection. Pressing it, he heard a faint click.

Standing back he watched in amazement as the panelling swung back against the wall to reveal a narrow passage. His heart began to beat heavily with expectation, his eyes straining into the blackness of the passage beyond, his ears listening for a sound that would tell him Katherine was in there somewhere. The tension was agony and his nerves were raw as he stepped inside, now able to see a faint glow filtering out of a doorway further along. He hurried towards it and an overwhelming surge of relief flowed through him when at last his eyes beheld Katherine.

It was dim inside the room, so small there was scarcely room for the pallet on which she lay. At the sight of her pale face on the pillow, so still and lifeless, as if it had been carved out of delicate ivory, a wave of sickness swept over him, not only at the sight of her helplessness but because he had been unable to prevent it.

Although he had refused to admit it to himself, there had been times when he had thought he had lost her forever. Looking down at her, he was drawn by her sheer loveliness and a rush of warmth pervaded his whole being. He was swamped with emotion almost beyond his control, and suddenly he was down on his knees by her bed, her small lifeless hands locked in his, and all his nerve centres, numbed by despair over Margaret's death, were reawakened, betraying just how deeply he felt for Katherine.

With relief he saw the gentle rise and fall of her chest beneath the covers. She was unconscious but alive, thank God—although he knew there was no point in trying to wake her, for Forbes had clearly not administered the drug until after she had screamed. It would be some time before she woke. Picking her up gently in his arms, he carried her back into the room she had occupied earlier and laid her on the bed, looking up when the others entered. Seeing Forbes among them, he pulled himself upright, an icy rage in his heart.

'So, Forbes—she isn't here, you said. This is your work, I believe,' he said accusingly, indicating Katherine's inert form, his quiet voice like an unsheathed blade.

'She isn't dead, is she?' asked one of the men stepping forward in alarm.

'No, thank God. She's unconscious—drugged.'

'Drugged?'

'Yes. An opiate has been administered—which you know all about, don't you, Forbes, since you are the one who administered it? They were your pipes I saw downstairs, weren't they? Used for smoking opium, if I'm not mistaken.'

Lord Forbes was beginning to look discomfited by this unfortunate turn of events, his eyes darting too and fro uneasily, for he had truly believed Mistress

Blair would not be found. 'There is nothing secret or wrong in the habit of smoking opium. As you well know it is widely used in the Orient,' he blurted, 'where there is approval for its powers.'

'Yes, I know all about its powers,' growled Blake scornfully. 'I also know that, if administered incorrectly, a single overdose can lead to instant death. I doubt Sir Matthew knows of the purpose to which his house is being used—or that you have clearly commandeered the services of members of his household to assist you in your evil deed. It is fortunate for you, Forbes, that you are not facing a charge of murder. Abduction is a serious enough charge in itself.'

Lord Forbes tensed before Blake's wrath, but, infuriated and desperate at being caught before he had cornered his prey, and frustrated by Mistress Blair's failure to comply with his demands in time, he did not intend being arrested without first incriminating her in some way.

'Why—in doing so I might have saved her from making a fool of herself,' he sneered.

Blake's eyes narrowed. 'What the devil are you talking about?'

'Why—the priest—Father Edmund. Didn't you know?' He spoke slowly, enunciating each word, his lips forming a slow smile of satisfaction at the horror and doubt which was beginning to cloud Lord Russell's eyes.

'Know? Know what, damn you?' snarled Blake,

Forbes's faint, contemptuous smile adding to his rage.

'That they are enamoured of each other. It is not uncommon for a priest to fall for a pretty face, you know. And they did make their feelings for each other abundantly clear to anyone who happened to see them locked in each other's arms in the park. Although they did meet at an early hour—when the park was more or less deserted.'

In a couple of strides Blake was in front of him, his features transfigured with fury, finding anger a release from the dark suspicions Forbes's insinuations had raised in him.

'What did you say? How dare you slander either Mistress Blair or Father Edmund with your lewd accusations?'

'Come now, Lord Russell, why such anger? After all, Mistress Blair is nothing to you. You are not even her guardian.' Lord Forbes's eyes narrowed as a thought suddenly occurred to him and he smiled insolently. 'Or is your rage and valour inspired because you want her for yourself? If so, then why not marry her since the demise of Lady Margaret Tawney has left you free to do so?'

His words caused murder to flare in Blake's eyes. He looked gigantic in his rage, his fists white and bunched by his sides, which caused Lord Forbes's unease to return. Fearing he was to be the recipient of those fists, with a look of desperation, realising he had gone too far, he spun round, looking for a way of escape like a cornered animal.

He ran quickly towards the door but, aware of his intent, Blake's reaction was swift and he strode after him, seizing him by the shoulder and forcing him to abandon any hope he might have had of escape. Lord Forbes's violent instinct for self-preservation made him lash out at Blake, but Blake's lust for vengeance was so powerful it made him the stronger, and the next moment his fist smashed into the side of Lord Forbes's face, felling him to the floor.

Blake turned to the constables, his face contorted with demoniacal fury. 'Get him out of here. Take him out of my sight before I kill him. And make sure he doesn't escape.'

Without hesitation the two constables dragged Lord Forbes and the Indian woman away to spend the night in Highgate gaol. There was no doubt in any of the minds of those present that, after appearing before the magistrate the following day he would be sent to the Tower.

Alone in the room with Katherine, Blake moved towards the bed and stood looking down at her, thinking over Rowland Forbes's accusations regarding her and Father Edmund, and once again he was forced to ask himself what it was that drew them to each other. He discounted as ridiculous Forbes's implication that they were lovers, but there was no doubt in his mind that Katherine had made some impression on the priest.

Forbes had told him he had seen them locked in an embrace. How much truth was there in this? he asked himself. But then he told himself not to go jumping to conclusions and thinking the worst. He would not believe Forbes's accusations before Katherine had had a chance to speak. He must give her a chance to defend herself, for there could be a perfectly reasonable explanation to their meeting in the park.

Katherine seemed to float in and out of consciousness for a long time. It was like being in a fog, which she struggled desperately to pierce. The time passed in some kind of haze that had no meaning as she drifted in and out of darkness. She had the sensation of being afraid, so terribly afraid.

But then, merciful Lord, Blake was there and everything ceased to exist but him. His dark figure hovered above, silently regarding her, his handsome features drawn. She wanted to reach out and draw him down to her but it was strange because she couldn't move her arms. They were too heavy.

Blake was reaching out his hands to her, slowly, ever so slowly, and she so dearly wanted him to touch her, but then the face bending down to hers didn't resemble Blake at all—the man she loved.

No, this was Lord Forbes, whose countenance was fair, his eyes blue and ice cold and his lips formed in a cruel sneer. It was then in her delirium that she screamed and thrashed about in an attempt to ward off this terrible evil and then he was gone, leaving her body trembling violently. It was stilled when she experienced the pleasant sensation of being rocked and comforted in someone's arms.

Eventually Katherine was able to claw her way to the edge of the mist and she had a sense of waking out of an interminable nightmare. Her head ached and felt so heavy.

When she awoke the following morning to find herself in her own bed at Landale House she thought she must be dreaming, that her abduction and the time spent in that strange house as Lord Forbes's prisoner had never happened. But gradually, as the memories came flooding back, she realised it was all too real.

But how had she got here? She closed her eyes; when she opened them again it was to find the sunlight streaming into her room, with no sign of the night's violent storm in which Blake, having borrowed one of Sir Matthew Mayhew's carriages, had brought her back to Landale House.

Amelia was standing beside the bed, smiling down at her. The nervous strain of Katherine's disappearance showed clearly on her face.

'Amelia! How did I get here?'

'Blake found you and brought you back.'

'Blake,' Katherine murmured, closing her eyes with a long, tired sigh. 'So—I wasn't dreaming after all.'

Sinking down onto the bed, Amelia took one of

her hands in her own. 'I can't tell you how dreadfully anxious we have been, Katherine. We were all out of our minds with worry. We had no idea what could have happened to you—who could possibly have had a hand in your disappearance—not even the smallest clue. It was as if the devil had carried you off.'

Katherine grimaced. 'He did. Lord Forbes is the devil incarnate.'

'We had no idea where to start looking for you—if you were alive, even. When our hopes were beginning to dwindle, Blake arrived from Ludgrove Hall.'

'Did—did he think that I was dead?'

'No. He never had a moment's doubt. He absolutely refused to consider it, rejecting the very idea. But you know Blake, Katherine. Even if he had, he would have his tongue cut out rather than admit it. He would not give up on you—refusing all rest—becoming like a man possessed in his determination to find you.'

Katherine's eyes clouded with tears and her heart soared with joy at this revelation by Amelia. For Blake to show such concern for her well-being told her that he must care for her after all.

'I am so sorry, Amelia. I did not mean to give you all such a fright. I—I must thank Blake for rescuing me. I owe him more than I can express. What has happened to Lord Forbes?'

Amelia's expression tightened at the mention of Katherine's abductor. 'He has been arrested and, I hope, thrown into the Tower by now—where he will languish until he is brought to trial—when he will be exposed for abduction.'

For a moment Katherine stared blankly at Amelia's kindly, anxious face and then, still under the effects of the drug, she broke down and wept bitterly, all the anguish and fear which had accumulated inside her coming out, her body racked with terrible sobs.

Moved by her terrible distress, Amelia edged closer to her, taking her in her arms and cradling her head against her, as if she were a child.

'Oh, Katherine, my dear—that's it—weep all you like. The pain will go away. You're safe now. We'll look after you and Lord Forbes will never touch you again,' she said fiercely as she continued to rock her in her arms.

As Katherine's tears subsided, bit by bit she told Amelia, who listened to her with an imperturbable calm, of her abduction, of how Lord Forbes had drugged her and her imprisonment—of how he had constantly insisted that she would marry him, come what may, revealing all the things that had hurt her, for it was necessary that Amelia knew the full extent of her suffering. There was only one thing she did not mention and that was his threat concerning Father Edmund—to expose him if she did not comply to his demands—for until she knew he was safe she thought it best to keep this to herself.

'The man is indeed a monster and will get what he deserves.' Amelia held Katherine at arm's length

and looked at her gravely. 'Katherine, forgive me if
I uncover unpleasant recollections by my imperti-
nence, for what I am about to ask you is of a delicate
nature—but—I must ask you. Did Lord Forbes
touch you in any way? Did he—?'

Katherine shut her eyes, feeling sick with anger
and disgust. 'I am aware of what you're about to ask,
Amelia,' she interrupted fiercely, 'and the answer is
no. No, he did not. I am a virgin still. But I feel
violated, nevertheless—as if he had raped me. The
manner in which he treated me was barbarous.
Mercifully, unlike the time at the inn, he was more
interested in obtaining my money than he was my
body. But had he wanted that then he would have
had to take me by force. If he beat me and starved
me, I would never have given in.'

Katherine turned her head away from Amelia as
fresh tears filled her eyes. There was only one reason
she would have complied with Lord Forbes's
wishes—to save the life of her brother.

But she dare not let her mind dwell too long on
this, for in her panic and fear, resulting from her
ordeal at the hands of Lord Forbes, she was
swamped with tormenting dread and despair that, as
a result of refusing to marry him, she might somehow
have played a part in her brother's downfall, and
that she would never see him again. She was terrified
that Lord Forbes, in his desperation to save his own
neck—and his desire for revenge—would reveal
where he was hiding.

CHAPTER ELEVEN

AFTER the physician had been to see Katherine, declaring her to be fit and well considering her ordeal, and that the effects of the drug would soon wear off, Blake knocked on the door of her room and entered. When he saw Katherine propped up against the pillows, the tears still wet and glistening on her cheeks, his breath caught in his throat and he was hard put to restrain himself from going to her and gathering her up into his arms, but he could see that she was making a concerted effort to be brave. She had been through a terrible ordeal and her nerves were strung tight—any strain might cause her to snap.

With an effort he restrained the urge to move close to her. She looked at him directly, without smiling, with gravely questioning eyes. Amelia rose and met her brother halfway into the room, laying to rest his worst fears by telling him quietly that Katherine was all right. She had not been violated.

The dark rage Blake felt, that Katherine had been made to suffer so, was at last overshadowed with relief, for that had been his greatest fear. He moved closer to the bed and stood looking down at her.

'I—I must thank you for coming to my rescue,'

Katherine said weakly. 'I was so afraid that no one would find me.'

'Thank God you are safe now and that villain is locked up.' Blake turned his head away to hide his feelings, the emotions her delicate loveliness evoked in him—weakening him. She would never know the tortures he had endured on her behalf. The image of all the indignities heaped on her defenceless body by Forbes had almost driven him to distraction.

Katherine looked at him with concern. He looked strained, his face seemed thinner and his mouth had taken on a sterner set. Remembering what Lord Forbes had told her, of Lady Margaret's demise, in a lightning flash of understanding she reached out tentatively and touched his hand lightly with her fingers.

'Oh, Blake, forgive me for all the distress I've caused you. I—I know about Lady Margaret and— and I am so terribly sorry. You had enough to contend with without my disappearance. I wish I could have spared you.'

Blake smiled softly. 'None of it was your fault. You weren't to know of Forbes's evil scheme to abduct you a second time.'

'How did you know where to look for me?'

'We received a note telling us.'

'A note? Who sent it?'

Blake shrugged. 'It was unsigned. I'd like to know who it was so that we could thank them.'

'How strange. Where was the place I was taken to and kept prisoner?'

'Highgate. The house was called Wycliffe Manor and is the home of Sir Matthew Mayhew—who happens to be a close friend of Lord Forbes. Sir Matthew is a merchant with the East India Company and is away at present. He is expected to be gone for some considerable time. The Indian woman and the elderly servant have been left at Wycliffe Manor as caretakers until he returns.'

'I see,' murmured Katherine. 'Then that explains the Indian woman's presence and the exotic strangeness of the house. What will happen to her?'

Blake shrugged. 'As to that I cannot say—not knowing how large a part she played in your abduction. I strongly suspect that she had no choice but to do as Forbes ordered. No doubt she will be imprisoned until the trial.'

'I see. What do you know of the drug Lord Forbes used to render me senseless? Is it harmful?'

'If administered incorrectly then it can be. But you need not concern yourself. The physician has assured us that although you have been physically weakened it is only a temporary state. As soon as the effects have worn off then there is no reason for you to remain in bed.'

'What was it? Did he say?'

'He believes it was a concoction called laudanum, whose principal ingredient is opium.'

'Opium? I believe I've heard of this. Isn't it grown somewhere in the Far East?'

Blake nodded. 'Yes, although it is extremely limited in Europe—but I should think Sir Matthew can come by it easily enough on his travels—which Forbes obviously obtains from him. And it seems,' he said with some amusement, 'if the smell and the opium pipes I noticed in the house are anything to go by, he has acquired the habit of smoking it. Although, come to think of it, he admitted as much himself—which would explain why he seems to be half out of his mind at times,' he grinned.

'Ugh, how utterly distasteful,' Katherine grimaced. 'After having it forced upon me—and having suffered its horrendous, hallucinating effects—I cannot for the life of me imagine how anyone can take it voluntarily. What will happen to him?'

'The villain took you against your will, and the base methods he used—violence and drugs—will sit heavily upon him.'

'Amelia tells me that you went to Ludgrove Hall before returning to London. How did you find things there?'

'Much the same as when you left.'

'And Matilda? How is she?'

'Missing you,' he said, smiling softly. 'Although there is a young man in the offing, I believe.'

'Of my aunt's choosing, I don't doubt,' uttered Katherine with irony. 'How is my aunt?'

'Much the same.'

'And angered, no doubt, because I haven't found myself a husband yet.'

'It was mentioned,' he said with a sudden twinkle in his eyes. 'But you can rest assured, Katherine, that I set her mind at rest by telling her there are many eligible young gentlemen, all vying with each other for your hand—and that it is only a matter of time before you make up your mind as to which one you will choose.'

A tremor ran through Katherine when he spoke her name and she smiled softly, gazing wonderingly into the dark depths of his eyes. 'How good it is to hear you speak my name. Is there a reason for this sudden change of heart?'

'Aye, minx,' he laughed, 'since you took to calling me Blake. And,' he murmured, his eyes full of tenderness, the sort of tenderness Katherine had despaired of ever seeing when he looked at her, 'I do agree with you. I, too, think it is high time we dispensed with the ridiculous formality between us.'

The pallor of Katherine's face disappeared beneath a delicate flush and she looked up, startled, at the amusement dancing in his dark eyes, for she had not realised that she had dispensed with the formality. 'Have I? Oh—forgive me—I was not aware of it.'

'There is nothing to forgive. I was glad to hear it.'

As they continued to talk Blake saw that all Katherine had endured was written clearly on her face. Her pallor returned, and the haunted look in her eyes bore testimony to the terrible experience she had lived through. She told him a little of her ordeal but she was careful to avoid any mention of Father Edmund, and Blake, sensing this, postponed the inevitable questions.

People listened in horror and stunned disbelief as news came to them of the outbreak of rebellion in Ireland. The reasons were deeply rooted in the past, and since the death of the Earl of Strafford and the breakdown of his administration in that unhappy land, the populace of England heard of British settlers being barbarously massacred in their thousands by discontented Irish Catholics, who had long smarted under English dominance and had been driven desperate by the injustices they suffered.

The conviction was that the rebellion was part of a Catholic conspiracy, and that priests were generally the ringleaders, going about the country, working among fellow Catholics and stirring them up to rebel against the English. Pamphlets that poured from the presses gave details of Catholic atrocities that turned people's stomachs.

These horrendous acts of violence perpetrated against the English settlers in Ireland raised the political situation and public excitement in England to fever pitch, and measures against Catholics in England were prosecuted with new vigor. In their abhorrence of popery the odium of the populace was thrown upon the papists. They were rounded up, tormented, interrogated and imprisoned.

Having recovered from her ordeal at the hands of Lord Forbes Katherine heard these stories with growing alarm. She had heard nothing from, or about, her brother, and she thought she would go mad with the strain of not knowing how he fared. Day after day she heard of fresh arrests, of priests being dragged before the courts and imprisoned, until, at last, her worst fears were realised. Blake, having just come from Westminster, was met by Amelia in the hall. He was not aware of Katherine's presence, for she hung back in the shadows.

Amelia greeted him eagerly. 'What news is there, Blake?'

His dark countenance was grim as he handed his cloak and gloves to a footman. 'The usual riots around Whitehall and in the Palace yard—with Catholics being hounded and rounded up.' He sighed deeply, looking gravely at his sister. 'The worst of it is that Father Edmund has been arrested and imprisoned.'

Katherine received this terrible news in silence, without any warning, and the impact of it struck her like a whip, causing her heart almost to stop beating. As blood flowed back into her veins she stepped into the light, white and trembling. Gazing straight ahead she moved towards them, fixing Blake with a stricken look.

'Imprisoned, you say? Where is he?'

'In Newgate,' he said gently. 'I'm sorry to have to be the bearer of such tragic news.'

She nodded slightly, swallowing hard. 'What will happen to him?'

'As to that—no one can say.'

Anguish tightened Katherine's heart and tears caused by her sudden desire to weep misted her eyes. She fell silent, then bowed her head, turning from them.

'Pray—excuse me. I must go to my room.'

Deeply concerned and curious by Katherine's reaction to the news about Father Edmund, Amelia watched her go. 'I must go to her,' she murmured, about to go after her, but Blake put a restraining hand on her arm.

'No. I will,' he said curtly, frowning deeply. 'It is high time the extent of Katherine's feelings towards this Catholic priest was made clear.'

On entering her room, he dismissed Rose and moved to where Katherine stood perfectly still, staring into the flames of the fire. She did not turn her head but sensed his presence.

'I'm sorry if my behaviour seemed odd, but news of Father Edmund's imprisonment came as quite a shock to me.'

'Clearly. Father Edmund!' said Blake with bitter emphasis. 'How anguished you sound when you speak of him. I feel you have involved yourself enough with this priest, Katherine. He is not the only priest incarcerated in Newgate.'

'I know,' she said sadly. 'But he is the only one that I care about.'

Her words caused a deep frown to crease Blake's brow as resentment and jealousy flared inside him. Grasping her shoulders, he turned her round to face him and Katherine shrank before his angry gaze, loaded with suspicion. He thrust his face close to hers so that she could feel his warm breath on her cheeks.

'So—it is true. There is more to this. Tell me what it is you feel for him—for it is not just kindness or pity that causes this concern for his well-being? Nor is it the tragic tale of a girl falling in love with a man who cannot return the sentiment because he is bound to the church by vows of chastity. No—it is something deeper—something warmer than that. What is it, Katherine? And what precisely was the reason why you went to meet him in the park?'

Katherine paled, staring up at him, feeling trapped within his burning gaze, feeling his hands gripping her shoulders. 'You know about that? Who told you?'

'Forbes.'

'I should have known,' she whispered. 'He did witness our meeting that morning, but I swear to you, Blake, that I did not arrange to meet him. You must believe that.'

'Then what is it between you? Tell me?' he demanded, his face darkening.

'Father Edmund is my friend, Blake, and merits my compassion. It is right that I am concerned.'

Blake frowned. 'I am not wholly convinced, Katherine, for you have not known each other long enough to establish such a close friendship.'

Katherine sighed, prepared to endure his close questioning rather than reveal the truth of her relationship to Father Edmund, for still there was something inside her which obstinately prevented her from telling him.

In her anguish, she mistakenly thought Blake's anger was caused by her close association with Father Edmund, but in truth Blake was in the grip of jealousy. Since the death of Margaret and the trauma of Katherine's abduction, he had come to realise just how much she meant to him, and he could not bear the thought of her being enamoured of any man but himself—be it courtier, king or priest.

'I cannot help what you think, Blake, but please tell me what will happen to him?'

'Because of his close association with Count Rossetti—and the fact that he is looked on favourably by the Queen—he will be called before the Commons and asked to take an oath on the King James Version of the Bible.'

'What does that mean?' asked Katherine in a small voice.

'That he must recognise the Sovereign as lawful and rightful King—repudiating the papal claim.'

Katherine blanched, for she could not envisage her brother doing this. 'And if he should refuse?'

Blake shook his head. 'That is not for me to say.'

She swallowed hard. 'He—he could hang, couldn't he?'

'Katherine,' Blake said gently, his features softening in the hope of placating her, 'few priests have been put to death in recent years. Conditions for Catholics improved greatly in England after the marriage of the King to Henrietta Maria, you know that.'

Katherine smiled with irony. 'I do not delude myself with that. Since the convening of Parliament those halcyon times have ended. In the light of what happened in Ireland I have heard the people in the streets baying for the blood of Catholics. The popularity of the Queen is sadly diminished and she is surrounded by hostility. Her royal servants have been exiled and she and her attendants are living like prisoners while the King is in Scotland.

'What chance does Father Edmund have in Newgate? He is alone at the mercy of other prisoners, and his gaolers, who will treat him as less than vermin. They will torture him, I know, regardless of the fact that he had no part in the rebellion in Ireland—his crime being that he is a Roman Catholic priest, who chose to live his life serving God.'

'Take heart, Katherine. He may take the oath. Some do.'

'And in doing so he will die as surely as if they

had hanged him, for he will not be set at liberty. I am not ignorant as to what it is like in Newgate, Blake. Father Edmund will die of the vile conditions he will be forced to endure there.'

'It is true that in the past those priests who suffered death might have saved their lives had they taken the oath, and those who did were left to languish in prison. But there is a chance that if Father Edmund does this then he will be banished from England.'

'Then, for his sake, I pray he will take the oath.'

Blake did not tell her that the ones who had taken the oath had brought on themselves the condemnation of Rome, that the denunciation of the Pope had proved infinitely far worse than death, and that, in consequence, they were deposed and shunned by fellow Catholics.

Again he placed his hands on her shoulders and looked deep into her eyes. 'I appreciate the ardour with which you spring to his aid, Katherine but, believe me, there is nothing that can be done. His life is in his own hands. For conscience' sake, I doubt his noble and pious heart will allow him to take the oath—but, for your sake, I pray that he will.'

He turned and left her then, cursing himself for being a fool, for he still did not know the reason—and neither did he understand—her devotion to the priest.

Alone, Katherine paced the carpet in her room as she thought fervently what could be done to save her brother. There must be something she could do. He must be persuaded to take the oath at all costs. She summoned Rose to her, a light of decision in her eyes, for she had made up her mind to see her brother herself. However, whether or not the Master Keeper of Newgate gaol would allow her to do so was a different matter.

'Come, Rose,' she ordered. 'Get your cloak. We are going out—and not a word to anyone about where we are going. Do you understand? If anyone should ask, we are merely going for an airing in the park.'

'Where *are* we going?' inquired Rose with growing apprehension.

'Newgate gaol,' answered Katherine, stuffing a small leather purse with coins with which to bribe the keeper, and placing it in the pocket of her skirt beneath her cloak.

Rose stared at her mistress in genuine astonishment, alarmed by her excited state. 'Newgate gaol?' She could not keep the note of fear out of her voice, for its very name conjured up hideous images in her mind.

'Yes. I'm going to try and see Father Edmund myself. I only hope I have enough money with which to bribe the keeper into allowing me to see him.'

Rose had been Katherine's maid for so long that there was little she did not know about her, but that she should show so much interest in a priest she strongly disapproved of, and she was shocked that she should even consider entering Newgate gaol to see him. It just wasn't natural.

Katherine could not repress a shudder when she stood in the grim shadow of the tower above the gate of Newgate gaol which spanned the street. Leaving Rose inside the coach, she climbed out, being met by an unkempt-looking guard who had been lounging by the gate. Slipping a coin into the man's grimy hand, she asked to see the Master Keeper. Grinning unpleasantly, the guard slipped the coin into his jacket pocket and took her to the Master Keeper, who turned out to be equally as unkempt, an ignorant, surly-looking individual.

When Katherine told him who it was she wished to see, he was somewhat surprised by her request and, after spitting noisily on the ground, flatly refused—until he saw the size of the purse in her hand and heard the irresistible clink of coins. A greedy sparkle entered his cold little eyes as he pocketed it. Picking up a heavy bunch of keys, he handed them to a turnkey, telling him to take the lady to see the priest in the Stone Hold. Not that she could stay long, mind, for the priest was no ordinary prisoner. He was under orders not to let anyone see him—but seeing as the lady looked quite desperate, and was clearly in a position to make the priest's stay in Newgate more comfortable, he leered, then he could see no reason why not.

'Where is he?' Katherine asked, finding it difficult to hide her revulsion for the man.

'Down in the Stone Hold—stinking, dismal and dark it is,' he rasped, throwing her a challenging look. 'A lady of quality, like yourself, might not have the stomach for it.'

Drawing a deep, determined breath, for already the foetid rotten air had assailed her nostrils, Katherine stepped forward. 'I'll stand it. Just let me see the prisoner.'

'As you like.'

Muffled in her cloak Katherine followed the turnkey, trying to keep her eyes fastened on his back so as not to see the full horror of this place. Ventilation was almost non-existent and the dank, stale air hit her in the face almost knocking her backwards. Even covering her nose with a handkerchief dipped in lavender water did nothing to lessen the smell.

She heard the sound of clanking chains from inside the cells that she hurried past, feeling sure they must be inhabited by demons. The prison housed murderers, debtors, thieves—the cream of London's criminal underworld. Criminals who could afford to pay for privileges were allowed to sleep in less undesirable parts of the appallingly overcrowded gaol. Every day felons died of the virulent fevers which often emptied the cells quicker that the carts bound for Tyburn.

Katherine looked about her with horror and distaste, her eyes beginning to smart with the effects of smoke from the sea-coal fires, around which felons huddled for warmth. She continued to follow the turnkey—hearing a varied assortment of voices, groans, curses, laughter, even, which sounded hideous in this hell hole—down a steep stairway, which seemed to plunge into the bowels of the earth, having to take the utmost care not to slip on the narrow stone steps by holding on to the damp, decaying wall, convinced she was descending into hell itself.

Eventually she came to what she thought must be the Stone Hold, which was underground and where no daylight could penetrate. It was a place that the turnkey took great delight in telling her had been where Roman Catholic martyrs had been incarcerated during the last century. In the dim yellow light Katherine saw it was a stinking, dismal place where the prisoners, having no beds, were compelled to sleep on the stone floor, surrounded by stagnant pools of water, enduring great hardship.

Katherine's eyes scanned the thin gaunt faces for the one she knew. It was his fair hair she saw first. Her brother sat leaning against the wall with his head bowed and his eyes closed. He came awake at once when the turnkey went to him and kicked his leg roughly, telling him he had a visitor, before turning from him and growling to Katherine that he'd be back soon.

Thinking Katherine was some kind of mirage, Father Edmund could do nothing but stare at her in amazement. Katherine fell to her knees beside him, noticing with horror the heavy iron shackles around his ankles, the chain fastened to the wall, cruelly restricting his movements and preventing any escape. Already he was showing signs of incarceration. His clothes were dirty and his normally clean-shaven face was showing a growth of beard. But neither the horror of his surroundings nor his appearance could detract from the youthful glow of his eyes when they lighted on Katherine.

'You!' he gasped, gripping her hands in his. 'This is madness. You should not have come here.'

'Forgive me—I had to. I don't have much time, Edmund. The turnkey will be back in a few minutes. Oh, why did you not escape to France? Why?'

'Because I discovered you were missing, Katherine. I could not leave until I knew you were safe.'

Katherine stared at him in wonder. 'You waited for me?'

'Yes. I suspected immediately that Lord Forbes had something to do with your abduction. Knowing of his close friendship with Sir Matthew Mayhew, who was out of the country, and that Lord Forbes often stayed at Wycliffe Manor, and after doing some investigating of my own, and speaking with Sir Matthew's elderly servant whom I happened to meet one day at the Angel Inn at Highgate, I discovered that I was right—that Lord Forbes was indeed staying there with a young lady. I was convinced that the young lady he spoke of was you.'

'Edmund—did you send Blake the note telling him where he could find me?'

'Yes. I was sorely tempted to try rescuing you from that man's clutches myself, but thought better of it. I knew Lord Russell stood a far better chance than I of freeing you.'

'And tell me—was it Lord Forbes who informed on you?'

'Yes, I believe so.'

'Dear Lord,' whispered Katherine. 'Then it is all my fault. If you had not been waiting for me, you would have left the country—and if I had given in to Lord Forbes's demands and agreed to marry him, you would not be here now. You see, he—he saw us together that morning in the park and drew his own vile conclusions. He threatened to expose your whereabouts if I did not agree to marry him. Oh, Edmund, I should have listened to him.'

'No Katherine,' he said fiercely, gripping her hands tightly, 'do not think like that. None of this is your fault. I am relieved Lord Russell found you safe and well, that you did not give in to Lord Forbes's scurrilous demands on account of me. But you did not tell him of our relationship, did you?'

She shook her head. 'No.'

He sighed with relief. 'Thank goodness. Now—tell me, why are you here? There is a reason other than just to see me, isn't there?'

'Yes. I came to ask you to take the oath of allegiance, Edmund.' Feeling his body stiffen beside her, she gripped his hand fiercely. 'You must. It is your only chance.'

Her brother spoke with gravity. 'Your concern touches me deeply. But, my dear, you do not know what you ask. I cannot take the oath.'

'But you must. They will torture you. They will kill you. Oh, Edmund—I cannot bear to think of it.'

Edmund drew her closer, neither of them conscious of the curious stares or sniggerings of the other prisoners, who obviously found this kind of behaviour between a priest and a beautiful woman unorthodox.

'Listen to me, Katherine. I know I shall be accused of treason, but I cannot in conscience recognise the substitution of the Pope by the King. It is an abomination to me. It is a demand of this approval and submission that I cannot give. Even if I took the oath my confinement might become easier, but I would not be set at liberty. Better to die than to spend my life incarcerated here.'

'But there is just a chance that, if you take the oath, when the King returns from Scotland then we could ask him to use his royal prerogative. You may be released on condition that you leave the country.'

'And then where will I go? Anyone who takes the oath is condemned by Rome. I am not a heretic and nor did I plot against the state or deny any doctrine of the Christian faith but it seems I am to die for some kind of treason. And do not even think of approaching the King on my account, Katherine. His personal influence cannot save me. He cannot use his prerogative to reprieve priests as he has in the past. Parliament would not tolerate it.'

Katherine bowed her head over their hands still clasped together, placing her lips on his fingers as her tears washed over them. Disentangling them, her brother cupped her face gently in his hands, looking deep into her eyes.

'If it has to be then so be it. I shall die a faithful witness to the Catholic teaching which I have followed all of my life. To serve God is the only life I want. I am the most faithful servant of kings and princes, Katherine, but God's first of all. Tell me you understand this? That you will reconcile yourself to this? It is important to me that you do.'

She nodded. 'Yes—yes, I do, and I am deeply ashamed that I have asked you to do such an ignoble thing. Forgive me. But I cannot accept that you might die—so please understand why I must try to find a way to free you.'

He smiled. 'Of course. But, Katherine, my dear, dear sister, if it has to be then I ask you not to torment yourself with my death. Do not suffer for me. You have so much to live for—so much ahead of you. Take it and be thankful for this short time we have had together. It is more than I ever hoped for.'

The turnkey returned and Katherine left her

brother, her heart heavy within her; she was fiercely determined to do all in her power to enable his escape. But, as she journeyed back to Landale House, she could not rid herself of the overriding fear of hopelessness and despair that haunted her, that grew more agonising with each gaping mile the carriage took her away from her brother's prison.

What could she do? she asked herself desperately. She had to seek help for she could not possibly open those prison gates alone. There was only one man she could turn to in her desperation—only one man who could help her—and that man was Blake.

Where have you been?'

CHAPTER TWELVE

AMELIA and her husband were not at home when
Katherine arrived back at Landale House. Rose
disappeared to the domestic quarters and Katherine
went in search of Blake. Having only just returned
from the docks himself, and being told by the
servants that Mistress Blair had gone for a drive in
the park with her maid, in the light of her recent
abduction he was at first perturbed and anxious, and
then angry, which increased as the minutes ticked
by, for it was growing dark. He had a creeping
suspicion that the park had been the last place she
had intended going to when she had set out.

When she eventually returned and entered the
drawing room, his face expressed relief and a fierce
joy that she was back safe and unharmed from
wherever it was she had been, but then he recol-
lected himself and strode towards her with an
expression of violent exasperation, reaching out and
gripping her shoulders.

'Where the devil have you been?' he demanded.

At the sight of so much anger Katherine almost
took flight. Never before had she seen Blake in such
a towering rage. 'I—I went to the park,' she lied.

'So you would have everyone believe,' he thundered. 'You went nowhere near the park. It may have escaped your notice but it is almost dark. Where have you been?'

Katherine looked at him steadily, preparing herself for a fresh tirade, knowing the moment of truth had come—that it could no longer be avoided.

'I—I went to Newgate gaol.' She quailed before Blake's hard stare of disbelief.

'You went to Newgate? So—at last we have the truth. I must say that I suspected as much but hoped that not even you would be foolish enough to do anything so stupid—dangerous, even. And did you succeed in getting in? Did you offer a substantial enough bribe to satisfy the keeper into letting you see the priest?'

Katherine nodded dumbly.

'Dear Lord,' said Blake incredulously.

'But I had to,' she burst out in a voice quivering with emotion. 'Don't you understand? I had to.'

'But why? In God's name, why? Tell me, Katherine?' he demanded, his hands tightening on her shoulders. 'What is it that exists between you and Father Edmund? It goes deeper than friendship—that is plain.'

Katherine raised her face imploringly to his, tears of despair misting her eyes, half out of her mind with fear of what his reaction would be when he knew the truth.

'Don't you know?' she cried. 'Can you not see when you look at us both? Are you still as blind as I was when I first came to London and saw him at Whitehall that day? Have you not looked at us together? Seen the resemblance?'

Blake stared at her, a sudden dawning in his eyes as he realised what she was trying to tell him. Before the thought had formulated in his mind, she spoke with all the passion of hopelessness and despair.

'He is my brother, Blake. My half-brother. He is of my own flesh and blood. Now do you see why I must do all in my power to help him? I cannot abandon him to his fate.'

Blake's hands dropped to his sides. All trace of anger had vanished from his expression but his face remained tense as he realised what the implication of this could mean—of the dangers to herself during these troubled days.

'Your brother? Yes,' he murmured, 'you are right—I have been blind. I should have seen it myself. At least this explains your strange behaviour where Father Edmund is concerned—and why, after not being seen for some time, he suddenly appeared when you arrived in London. But why did you not tell me of this sooner? Why have you allowed me to believe it was some kind of affair of the heart that drew you together?'

'But how could I know you thought that?' she cried in dismay, her tears beginning to spill over and course slowly down her cheeks. 'I did not know for certain that he was my brother until that morning in the park when he sought me out. I did not even know I had a brother until my aunt told me—the day I came and asked you to intercede on my behalf and persuade her to allow me to go to London with Amelia. Do you remember that day, Blake? Do you?'

'Yes,' he said softly, a deep tenderness in his eyes, remembering their kiss and how it had felt to hold her in his arms. 'It is a day I shall never forget. It is the day I kissed you. So—that was what had upset you. Oh, Katherine, why did you not tell me?'

'I did not tell you because my aunt told me not to. Also, because my mother was a Catholic. I knew of your aversion to anyone of that faith, and because of the resurgence of hate in the country against any Catholic, I believed it was in my own best interests to keep silent.'

Blake sighed, placing his hand gently beneath her chin and tilting her face to his. Katherine saw his expression change. In a voice that was suddenly sympathetic and understanding, he said, 'You little fool. Didn't you realise that I already knew your mother was a Catholic? My father told me years ago.'

With a wildly beating heart, Katherine stared at him. 'You knew all the time?' she whispered.

'Yes—and I have to tell you that after my father told me I quite forgot about it. So, there, Katherine—that is how little it meant to me. And as to the Catholic faith as a whole—well—I must say that I no more wish to be dictated to by the

Presbyterian Kirk of Scotland than I do the Pope of Rome and that I wish for nothing better than a peaceful coexistence with my neighbour—whatever his religion happens to be.

'And there is something else you should know,' he uttered in a strangely quiet voice which made Katherine's pulses quicken, for his handsome face was grave and unsmiling and he was looking at her as he had never looked at her before.

'Oh?'

'Yes. Contrary to what you believe, my dear Katherine, I love you too much to let the fact that your brother is a Roman Catholic priest come between us. I would not care if he were the Pope himself.'

Katherine stared at him in bewildered disbelief. He was looking down at her as if he had never seen her before, as if his eyes could not get enough of her. She drew in her breath sharply, aware that something was happening between them—something wonderful and glorious.

'But—Blake—what are you saying . . .?'

Cupping her face in his firm hands so that the candlelight lit up her magnificent eyes, he looked at her, his dark eyes burning with all the love and passion Katherine had despaired of ever seeing there.

'What I am saying is that I love you, Katherine,' he said softly, 'and that is the truth of it. I love you more than I ever thought it was possible to love any woman—and yes, may God forgive me—even Margaret, and it was because of my betrothal to her that I could not disclose to you how I felt—for I did not have the right to love you. I knew before she died how I felt, but I had promised to marry her. I was prepared to enter into a most solemn contract in the sight of God and man, loving not my intended bride but another woman—which would have been a sin in itself.

'But how could I have believed for one moment that I could live the rest of my life away from you? Each day would have brought fresh torment when I imagined you in the arms of another man. But how I wish the situation could have been resolved in some other way—without Margaret's death.'

Katherine's tears ceased to flow. Waves of great joy swept over her and inwardly she prayed that this marvellous moment would go on for ever. 'Oh, Blake,' she sighed, 'if only you knew how I have prayed for you to say those words to me. I have loved you for so long and so much that sometimes it has been too great for me to bear. I have always loved you—ever since I first saw you when I was just a girl.'

Gently Blake laid his hands on Katherine's shoulders and drew her to him, his strong arms folding round her and drawing her close to his hard chest as his head descended to hers.

'Say you love me again?' he murmured. 'Let me hear it again?'

For answer she put her arms about his neck and turned her face up to his and offered him her lips, feeling his mouth on hers, firm and demanding, with all the pent-up passion of something long desired but which they thought would always be denied them. There was no tenderness in that kiss. It was hard and violent, filled with desperation, and for a moment time seemed to stand still for them as they were swept along on a savage tide of love.

Katherine clung to him, her passion equalling his own so that everything and everyone was forgotten in their desperate need for each other. Blake's mouth moved from her lips to her eyes, her throat, and back to her lips, and again they kissed as if to quench this demanding thirst which, even when they thought they had drunk their fill, remained unslaked.

When desperation ebbed, slowly they drew apart and looked—without fear or any obstacles between them—deep into each other's eyes, with silence all around them. Never had Blake known a love like this and he was reminded of how it had been with Margaret, with reticences and gentleness. Theirs had been a comfortable, close kind of friendship, but with Katherine it was so different. They shared an unashamed passion for each other. There would be no defences between them, no reserve.

Her face was still so close to his that he could see her beautiful black-lashed eyes dark with love, the soft down on her flushed cheeks, how her moist lips quivered and were parted slightly to reveal her teeth gleaming like pearls. He longed to taste once again the sweetness of those lips, to feel their softness, but time enough for that later.

At that moment a footman, having knocked on the door and told to enter by Blake, stood in the doorway and announced that Lord Soames had arrived, requesting to see Mistress Blair.

Before Katherine could tell him to show Lord Soames in, Blake stepped forward.

'Tell Lord Soames that Mistress Blair is not at home.'

When the footman had disappeared Katherine turned to him with a look of teasing reproach but, in truth, she had no wish to see or speak to anyone other than Blake at that moment. 'Really, Blake, I should have seen him. What will he think?'

'My love—I care not one way or the other. You are no longer on the marriage market and I shall let it be known. The only man you will receive from now on is myself, and very soon we shall set the seal on our love when we become husband and wife— but first we have the urgent matter of your brother to consider. Come,' he said, drawing her down beside him on to a sofa, 'and tell me about Father Edmund and how you discovered he was your brother?'

His words brought Katherine out of her cloud and down to earth with a feeling of guilt for having so easily forgotten her brother's desperate plight. With her hands in his she sat and faced him, trying to still the throbbing in her veins. She loved him so much but she must try not to think of her fiercely urgent desire for him to take her in his arms again, for his kiss, which a few moments before had wiped all thought of her brother from her mind. Blake was right. She must remain clearheaded at all costs in order to help Edmund.

Quickly Katherine told him all she knew, all her brother had told her of his life in France and Rome, of how he had come to England to find her.

'So—it seems you were not mistaken. It was your brother you saw in Appleby that day?'

'Yes, it was. He was there looking for me—to see me—to reassure himself that I was well taken care of. He did not know whether or not I had been told of his existence and so, to spare my feelings, not wishing to hurt or embarrass me in any way, he had no intention of approaching me. But is it not an abomination when a brother cannot make himself known to his sister—his crime being that he is a Catholic priest and could incrimiate her, even though she does not share his faith?'

'Sadly, that is the case. If it becomes known that Father Edmund is your brother, then attention would be drawn to you and that would not help matters. It would only make things worse, for you would be arrested and interrogated.'

'There must be something that can be done to help him. I cannot bear to see him in that place— shackled to the wall like a dog.' She hung her head with a crushing sense of guilt. 'It is my fault. It is all my fault. I am so dreadfully ashamed that I have unwittingly been the cause of his capture and imprisonment.'

'Hush, Katherine, you have nothing to blame yourself for. Lord Forbes is the one responsible for your brother being where he is, I know that. No one else.'

'But it is my fault,' she persisted. 'If I had agreed to marry Lord Forbes then none of this would have happened and my brother would be safe—across the water in France by now. Lord Forbes threatened to expose him but I would not listen. I prayed that the longer I held out against him the more chance Edmund would have of getting out of the country. It is my rejection of Lord Forbes which has brought my brother to this pass. Oh, Blake, how could I have brought so much misfortune on him of all people? It was he who sent you the note telling you where to find me.'

Blake nodded, not surprised by this. 'So—I should have known. When you saw him in Newgate did you ask him to take the oath?'

Katherine nodded. 'Yes. That was my reason for going there, but he will not take it.'

'That comes as no surprise to me.'

'He gave me no encouragement to hope and seems resigned to his fate.' She looked at Blake imploringly. 'What can I do, Blake? There must be a way to help him. I can pay for his release. Do you think one of the keepers can be bribed?'

Blake frowned, shaking his head firmly. 'No, Katherine. In Newgate gaol bribery can effect most things save liberty.' Seeing her stricken look, once again he drew her into an embrace. 'I promise you that I will do all in my power to help him. Now I know who he is, believe me, I desire his release as much as you do. But I beg of you—be patient. Wait until after the trial.'

'I cannot remain calm, Blake. After the trial may be too late.'

'Nevertheless, you must. To arrange his escape will be no simple matter and will require perfect planning if it is to have any possible chance of success. When we know the verdict we shall act quickly.'

'Very well,' she acquiesced. 'But meanwhile, is there anything we can do to make his imprisonment more bearable? He is in the most wretched place—the Stone Hold, they call it—deep underground. I know many of the prisoners pay for privileges—that prisons are places of profit for keepers and turnkeys alike.'

Blake nodded. 'I'll do my best to ease his suffering, Katherine. I promise.'

Content with this, Katherine nestled into his embrace, overcome with joy at the amount of assistance she had scarcely dared to hope for.

* * *

Blake had set the wheels in motion immediately in an attempt to secure the release of Father Edmund. He had gone to see the Queen at Oatlands to plead his case. Henrietta Maria had been deeply saddened by the priest's imprisonment but with deep regret had been powerless to help him. At one time, perhaps, but not anymore. He had not been the only priest Parliament had removed from her side. There was only one man who might still have had the power to help secure his release—King Charles, although his powers had been drastically diminished of late, and he was still in Scotland.

Katherine had been numb as she had awaited news of her brother—of the outcome of his trial. What if he were found guilty of treason for refusing to take the oath of allegiance and taken from Newgate to Tyburn and hanged? How could she bear it? Such thoughts as these, combined with her inability to help him, had lowered her spirits.

Those agonising days of waiting were over when Blake returned from Westminster one day, lines of worry etched on his face, and Katherine was instantly alert that something was wrong. She went towards him the moment he entered the hall, her two hands outstretched. Blake noticed how enormous her eyes were in her pale face, the dark circles of pain and grief making them look even larger.

'What is it, Blake? Tell me. It's bad news, isn't it?'

'Yes. The worst—but I expected no less.'

Katherine put her hands over her mouth in horror.

'No. Oh, no,' she whispered. 'Tell me. Do not spare me. Edmund refused to take the oath, didn't he? He—he has been condemned to die?'

Blake nodded, wishing he could spare her this torture. He took her cold hands in his own and drew her close. 'Yes, Katherine,' he said gently. 'He is to be executed.'

Because of the weight of grief she was struggling under, he did not tell her the full horror of her brother's sentence—that he was to be fastened to a hurdle and dragged through the streets to Tyburn, where he was to be hanged before having to suffer the full agony of being cut down while still alive, disembowelled and quartered. She was sufficiently unhappy without knowing that.

'Dear God,' she whispered. 'How can I endure it?'

Blake reached out and placed his hands firmly on her shoulders in an effort to inspire her with that same indomitable spirit he always associated with her, which had temporarily deserted her.

'Katherine, look at me,' he demanded fiercely, resisting the urge to shake her. 'You have to be strong for your brother's sake. You must maintain your courage.'

Katherine looked at him direct as gradually his words and the biting grip of his hands on her shoulders caused life to return to her brain and her body began to function after days of being drained of courage and all capacity for thought. Her instinct that she must fight on to help her brother revived in her.

'Yes, you are right. I must be strong. We must save him. But I fail to understand why he has to die, Blake? How can they condemn a man because he is steadfast in what he believes in?'

'It isn't that alone that has condemned him. Because of his friendship with Count Rossetti and his closeness to the Queen, it is believed that he might have known something of the circumstances concerning the Irish uprising.'

'But that is nonsense,' cried Katherine bitterly.

'That may be, but the uprising, which is said to have resulted in the massacre of hundreds of English settlers—and which has deepened the opposition already felt towards the Catholics in this country—is conceived to be a vast conspiracy emanating from England construed by the Queen and her cohorts. Rumours about the Queen's intrigues and appeals to Roman Catholic powers abroad in the past, have already inflamed public opinion. Credence has been given to the involvement of priests in the uprising by witnesses who claim to have overheard plots being made by them.'

'And, naturally, the populace—feeling such abhorrence towards anyone belonging to that sect—are all too ready to swallow anything. And it is because of this that my brother is to die,' Katherine said bitterly. 'They have no evidence that he took part in anything—but they are looking for a scapegoat to appease their anger—and who better than a Roman Catholic priest who is highly thought of by the Queen? What can be done, Blake?'

Katherine saw there was a deep and thoughtful look in his eyes, that a serious frown creased his brow. 'Come,' she said sharply. 'I know that look. You have a plan in mind. Tell me?'

Blake guided her into the drawing room, out of earshot of curious servants, closing the door behind them before he spoke.

'I intend to get him out of Newgate,' he said decisively, glad to see Katherine brighten visibly at his words. 'Although I have not seen him myself— the reason being that I want no one to associate me with him at this time—I have managed to make his time in Newgate more bearable.'

'How?'

'By sending enough money to the Master Keeper—anonymously, of course—asking him to see that Father Edmund be allowed the liberty of a cell above ground—and without shackles. This will prove convenient for what I have in mind later. Also, nothing can be done in that place without money, so I have seen to it that he has been given enough with which to bribe the turnkeys into providing him with extra food and warmth.'

Katherine was overwhelmed with relief to know Edmund was no longer being forced to exist in that miserable hole beneath the prison. 'That is good news, Blake. I can't tell you how grateful I am to you, that your time has been spent on my brother's account. But how did you get the money to him?'

'By recruiting the aid of another prisoner—Jack Nolan, who just so happens to be a member of the crew from one of our ships, who has been languishing in Newgate for several days now.'

'Why? What has he done?'

'When his ship docked after a voyage from the Indies, like all sailors who have been without drink and women for weeks on end, his first night on dry land was one for celebration. As is usually the case, the celebrating got out of hand and he became involved in a drunken brawl which resulted in the death of another sailor. He has been charged with murder.'

'What will happen to him?'

'He hasn't been taken before the sessions as yet— but doubtless he will be found guilty and will hang.'

Katherine paled, finding there was nothing she could say, for she felt that the sailor probably deserved his fate if he had killed a man—whereas her brother had killed no one and he was to die, also. Where was the justice in this?

'You said you intend getting Edmund out of Newgate. Tell me what you have in mind?'

'I've given the matter a great deal of thought. The day after tomorrow is a public hanging day, when prisoners to be hanged are taken from Newgate to Tyburn.'

Katherine gasped in horror. 'Not Edmund. He is not to die so soon?'

'No—calm yourself, Katherine. The day for his execution has not yet been decided—although it cannot be too far away, so we must act quickly. You have never seen a hanging day at Tyburn, have you?'

All the colour drained from Katherine's face as she envisaged the horror if it. The very name 'Tyburn', chilled her blood. 'No,' she whispered, 'and I pray God I never have to.'

'They are public holidays,' he explained, 'for it is considered that the sight of an execution will prove a deterrent to the multitude of spectators who attend. Sadly, it takes on the aspect of a fair day rather than a public hanging. You can imagine the amount of confusion in and around Newgate there will be on such a day. I consider this the time to act. I have enlisted the services of Jack Nolan to help me once I am inside.'

'Is he to be trusted?'

'Yes. None better.'

'Do you think you can save him?'

'I hope so. It is our only chance,' he said, averting his eyes quickly, but too late, for Katherine had seen the cloud of doubt darken his eyes.

Katherine, whose hopes had risen considerably, was forced to admit the horrifying prospect that it could all go disastrously wrong. She felt her throat go dry at the mere thought, and with a despairing groan she went to him, clinging to him. She felt his arms go around her, his warm breath in her hair. A tear rolled down her cheek, for at that moment she thought of nothing other than the mortal danger he would be placing himself in.

'I cannot let you do this,' she said, her head pressed against his chest. 'Not for me. Nothing must happen to you, for that I could not bear. If you do not succeed, they will hang you too.'

Blake's arms tightened around her. 'I have to do it, Katherine, for both our sakes—and for his. I have to save him from an unjust fate. If I do nothing then, his tragic captive figure will always be between us. We will succeed. We have to.'

Despite the hope his words held, they scarcely penetrated Katherine's mind. 'No—no. I cannot let you do this. It is madness—nothing but a forlorn hope.'

Blake gripped her arms, holding her away from him. 'You must not say that,' he said fiercely. 'If you think like that then we are doomed from the start.'

Before Katherine could utter one more word Blake stopped her mouth with a kiss, infusing into her all the force and passion of his love for her. When he raised his head he looked fiercely down into her tear-filled eyes.

'Before God, Katherine, I am going to get him out.'

The savage look of determination on his face, burning in his eyes, revived Katherine's failing hopes and breathed new spirit into her, making her feel deeply ashamed. How could she ever think of losing hope when Blake was by her side, willing to brave anything on her behalf?

She swallowed hard. 'Tell me what it is you have in mind, Blake? What can I do to help Edmund's escape?'

'Nothing. You must leave that part to me. No more questions. You will have to trust me.'

Yes, Katherine thought, she would trust him with her life. But what could he do? He would be one man alone against the solid might of Newgate gaol and its multitude of keepers.

As if reading what was going through her mind, Blake smiled. 'Don't worry. If everything goes to plan everyone will be too busy with the day's hangings to take much notice of what is taking place in your brother's cell. One of our ships will be sailing with the tide for the Indies on that day. With any luck your brother will be on board. The captain will have instructions to put in briefly at a port on the French coast.'

Katherine listened to him in amazement. He smiled once more. 'Don't worry,' he said softly, gathering her into his arms again. 'You will be able to say goodbye to him. I will tell you more when the time comes. Now, kiss me, Katherine—' his eyes took on a merry tuinkle as he attempted to relieve the tension inside her '—for I feel your kisses will give me the sustenance I am going to need if I am to relieve your brother of his captivity.'

Blake's lips were on Katherine's, giving her no time to object—not that she would have wanted to if he had. She abandoned herself to him, feeling the hardness of his male body pressed close to hers, and with a low moan she melted against him, robbed of her senses as she kissed him passionately, her whole body shuddering against his, feeling the rising of her desire for him grow almost beyond her power.

When she drew back she was amazed by her own sensuality, but Blake took it for what it was and was overwhelmed with tenderness for her, for, in contrast to himself, she was innocent of any experience. His eyes were languid as he looked down at her upturned face and he smiled slowly, for spirited and quarrelsome she might be, but in this he would have complete control.

At this point Amelia entered the room, taking in the scene at a glance, completely oblivious to what they had been discussing. Slowly Katherine disentangled herself from Blake's arms, not in the least embarrassed that they should be caught out in such an open show of affection.

Amelia swept across the room, smiling broadly, for she had been a bright-eyed observer of the situation developing between them for some time now—in fact, she had gone out of her way to encourage it—and she was absolutely delighted that they had neither the reason or desire to deny their love for each other any longer. It was good to see that the pain in Blake's eyes caused by Margaret's death had disappeared.

'Don't mind me,' she laughed. 'I did not mean to interrupt. You cannot conceive how happy I am for you both. I always knew you were meant for each other. The fact that you were always at each other's throats did not fool me for one minute. But I shudder to think what your lives will be like together—both strong-willed and determined to have your own way. Unless this means that from now on we are to be blessed with a more tranquil relationship between you both?' she queried, her eyes twinkling mischievously.

Blake grinned lovingly down at Katherine. 'No doubt she will continue to plague me with her quarrelsome, shrewish tongue, but it should make life stimulating enough—until I have taught her to curb it, that is.'

Katherine poked him in the ribs with teasing reproach. 'I will overlook that conceited remark— but I would hasten to say that I am no shrew, my lord, and I am only quarrelsome when provoked. And I will have you know that if you think you are to have it all your own way when we are wed then you are mistaken.'

'Then maybe I should seek a quieter, more subdued woman to be my bride,' he mocked jokingly.

'Aye—do that, my lord, and die of boredom into the bargain.'

Blake planted a kiss firmly on her lips, placing his

arm about her waist and drawing her close, serious once more. 'As if I could think of spending my life with anyone other than you. As soon as we are able we shall return to Ludgrove Hall and be married.'

The happy smiled faded from Katherine's face and Amelia's observant eyes saw in her expression that which suggested something like distress. Contemplating both their features she frowned curiously.

'I'm sorry—but I sense there is something amiss?'

Blake looked at her steadily. 'Aye—there is. I have just returned from Westminster and told Katherine of Father Edmund's sentence.'

'Yes. I have heard,' Amelia replied. ''Tis a terrible business. Such a nice young man and highly thought of by both the King and Queen. What a great pity he did not escape to the continent when he had the chance.' She looked from one to the other, her eyes narrowing suspiciously, for she had a creeping feeling that all was not well.

'But there is more to this, isn't there? What is it? Come—please do not be evasive, either of you. There is something I do not understand—but what I do know is that it has something to do with Father Edmund. Many of our acquaintances have been condemned to death for something or other over the years, but I do not remember this sadness. What is so different about Father Edmund, pray?'

'The sentence is unjust, Amelia,' Blake answered. 'I have no mind to see an innocent man die.'

'Then what will you do, Blake? What can you do?

I see no reason why you should endanger your own life for him—as I would any other condemned felon in Newgate for that matter. This man is a priest. He has been tried and condemned fairly.'

'Fairly? Oh, no, Amelia,' said Blake fiercely. 'You do not understand.'

'No—you are right—I don't,' she said sharply, her eyes darting from one to the other.

Katherine looked up at Blake, placing her hand gently on his arm. 'Tell her, Blake. She should know.'

He nodded. 'Very well.'

Quickly Blake told his sister all about Father Edmund being Katherine's half-brother—of how he had come to England to look for her and how surprised she had been, for the fact that she had a brother at all had remained unknown to her until her aunt had told her shortly before she had left Ludgrove Hall.

At first Amelia listened in a stunned silence which gradually became an imperturbable calm, for she now realised that, with Blake loving Katherine as passionately as he did, he felt duty bound to try and help her brother. But at what cost to himself? His life? When he had finished speaking she turned to Katherine, her face deathly pale.

'I am so sorry, Katherine. I knew nothing of this. But I see no reason why Blake should risk his life—for this is what it amounts to, isn't it, Blake?' His dark, blank expression told her that this was indeed so. 'You will not succeed. It will only result in the death of both you and Father Edmund. Why did you not say anything to me, Katherine, about Father Edmund being your brother?'

'I'm sorry, Amelia, but I could not—and, anyhow, I did not know myself until shortly before my abduction. Also, because of the harsh treatment being inflicted on the Catholics at this time, I did not wish to endanger any of you should it become known that my brother was a Catholic priest.'

Very much aware of her deep sadness, Blake drew her close. 'No matter what your opinion, Amelia, I have to try to save him.'

She nodded, swallowing hard. 'When?' she asked with difficulty.

'The day after tomorrow on the hanging day— when it will be a public holiday.'

'Yes—well—' sighed Amelia, knowing how useless it would be to argue with him, but she was not convinced that he was doing the right thing '—I suppose that will be as good a day as any other. But you must perceive the danger and take heed, for do not imagine for one moment that it will be an easy matter getting him out of Newgate alone, Blake. You will need help. But you must take care, for it is difficult to know who to trust in these days of suspicion and scheming.'

CHAPTER THIRTEEN

WHEN Blake arrived at Newgate, a large crowd had already gathered at the prison and along the street, peering in through the gates like a theatrical audience, seething and noisy, the sound reverberating between the walls of the houses and shops. He climbed out of the coach, glancing back to make quite sure the second coach was close by, empty except for the coach driver. When Father Edmund emerged from the prison dressed in the clothes Blake now wore, this was the coach that would whisk him away to the docks and the waiting ship.

The driver of the coach Blake had just alighted from had instructions to wait until the other coach had been gone for some thirty minutes before enquiring of the Master Keeper as to what could be keeping Lord Russell inside the prison. If all went to plan, the Master Keeper would be under the impression that Lord Russell had left some time since.

Blake approached the prison on foot, hearing the doleful tolling of the bell at St Sepulchre's which always tolled upon hanging days. The carts with the condemned prisoners were beginning to collect in the prison yard. There were three of them today,

263

three prisoners to each cart—a mixed bunch of men and women, young and old, some sitting on their coffins, others beside them. Some had their heads bowed in misery while others cast fearful glances at the seething crowd in the street which was hostile today, and as soon as the carts were sighted the prisoners were showered with a storm of missiles.

When the procession set out on its long journey to Tyburn it would be escorted by the City Marshal and constables, stopping at taverns along the way to allow the prisoners to partake of their last drink. Often the journey could take two hours or more, and by the time they reached Tyburn many were drunk when they were hoisted up to the gallows.

Taking advantage of the confusion Blake slipped into the prison yard, finding the Master Keeper in conversation with the prison chaplain who, on Blake's approach, moved away and climbed into one of the carts with the condemned to offer solace and prayers on their way to Tyburn.

The Master Keeper saw nothing unusual in Blake's request to see Jack Nolan—the sailor who had killed a man in a drunken brawl and was expected to hang—for it wasn't the first time the gentleman had paid him a visit. Remembering the large purse he had handed over, and receiving the same again, he had no objections and handed him over to one of the turnkeys.

Blake followed the turnkey inside the prison with its great thick walls. The very name of Newgate was enough to make one tremble. The turnkey unlocked iron gates, locking them again after they had passed through. They moved along a dimly lit stone passage, cold and dirty, passing the top of a flight of stairs leading down to the underground cells.

His face grim, his mind fixed on the task in hand, Blake was undaunted by this forbidding place. He followed the turnkey along dark corridors, taking care to keep his head lowered, his features in shadow, for it was important that the man would remember his elaborate garb—his scarlet suit and short swaying cloak, the wide-brimmed hat with swaying white plumes which covered his hair— rather than his features.

At last they entered the interior of Newgate gaol which Blake was sure was on the entrance of hell. He was met by the deafening clamour of a multitude of people, a cacophony of noise—shouting, singing, cursing, laughing, all attacking his ears at once. They passed through rooms crowded with men and women mixing freely with each other—a dreadful army of criminals who inhabited this accursed world—people from all walks of life and different classes—from gentlemen in faded finery to the lowest debtor. Hunger and cold were the lot of those who couldn't pay the turnkeys for food and warmth, while those more fortunate had grown fat on idleness.

The recent inmates to the gaol were down and dejected while others, the hardened criminals, were reconciled to the conditions so that it had become tolerable. Few gentlemen retained manners of good breeding and had fallen into the degenerate ways that were Newgate.

Finding Jack Nolan sitting dejectedly on a stool, the turnkey left Blake, eager to return to the spectacle of the condemned felons being carted off to Tyburn.

Jack Nolan was a tall, strongly built man, the skin of his face like weathered parchment as a result of many years spent at sea. He may have unintentionally killed a man in a drunken brawl but he was prepared to pay for it with his own life. Blake knew that above all else he was a man to be trusted, and seeing it as his only chance of procuring Father Edmund's escape, he had taken him into his confidence on his previous visit, telling him of his plan.

Jack thought he was mad to even attempt to get a man out of Newgate, but it was not for him to argue and so he agreed to assist him. After all, he had nothing to lose and his family, his wife and children, had everything to gain. When the hangman had done his work and his wife was widowed, Lord Russell, who was a gentleman and a man of his word, had promised to see they would be well taken care of— that they would want for nothing.

Jack glanced up when Blake approached. He rose. 'Why, my lord, you honour me with your visit,' he said for the benefit of others who were looking their way, for there were those who had been incarcerated for years, who had forgotten what a gentleman resplendent in such fine garb looked like. Such a visit was always an occasion for ribald curiosity.

Blake ignored the attention he had drawn to himself and, as he took Jack to one side, already people were beginning to turn away.

'Have you seen the priest? Spoken with him?'

'Aye.'

'He knows to expect me?'

Jack nodded. 'Come with me—and act casual, like, while we talk. 'Tis fortunate that he is in a cell on this landing and not too far away—but we do not want to attract too much notice to ourselves so we must be especially careful.'

They moved on down a dark corridor which to Blake seemed endless. It was with abject relief that they slipped unnoticed into Father Edmund's cell. He was sitting on the floor, leaning against the wall, but rose quickly and moved forward to greet them when Blake and his companion entered. In the dim light which came from a small window high up in the wall running with water, Blake could see that his clothes were torn and dirty, his face pale, his hair lank and hanging loose, and that he had lost weight as a result of his incarceration. Apart from these outward signs of discomfort and distress, Blake was relieved to see he remained physically fit and well.

'Lord Russell!' he exclaimed. 'Mr Nolan told me to expect you but I did not delude myself into believing you would get past the guards.'

'Money will attain anything in Newgate save freedom,' Blake replied. 'But it is my intention to deliver you from this wretched place.'

'How can you? It cannot be done.'

Blake smiled grimly. 'I would not be here if I did not think otherwise.'

'But the risk to yourself is too great. I appreciate what you are trying to do, my good sir, but you must leave me. I am comfortable enough—more so than most in this place. I believe—although my benefactor remains a mystery to the Master Keeper—that after speaking to Mr Nolan, I have you to thank for this—and for having me taken from that frightful dungeon I was thrown into at the beginning of my imprisonment. I cannot express the gratitude I feel. It is beyond words. But I have to say that your plan to get me out of here is foolhardy. Men have been condemned for less.'

'That I know. But I am already in your debt. It was you, was it not, who sent me the note informing me where Katherine could be found? Without that I shudder to think what could have befallen her at the hands of her abductor.'

Edmund fixed him with his steady penetrating gaze. 'It was important to me, too, that she was found safe and well.'

'I know that, also. I also know that your death cannot be right. A man should not die for his beliefs. I am not a Catholic—and nor could I be called a devout Protestant, but I do believe there should be more tolerance—that people of different faiths should be making friends, not denying each other. You must understand why I could not make it known that it was I who gave the money to have you moved from that hell hole, why I must deny any relationship with you.

'It is imperative that we are not seen together—not for myself—but in order to protect Katherine and my family, you understand? There are those who might conceive it their duty to punish them. However innocent they might be, no one would believe they had no part in your escape should we succeed. And Katherine must be protected at all costs, for she is your sister and the authorities would take some convincing that she is not of your faith.'

Edmund gazed at him steadily. 'So, she has told you that she is my sister?'

'Aye, she had to. She is to be my wife so there must be no secrets between us.'

'You love her?'

'More than my life.'

Edmund put out his hand and Blake gripped it hard in both his own. 'Then may you find great joy and comfort in each other,' Edmund murmured. 'I am glad, indeed you don't know how glad I am—how relieved it makes me feel to know that she will be taken care of.'

'That I guarantee. Now—come. We must make haste for there is no time to lose. The turnkey will be back shortly.' Blake immediately began unfastening his jacket.

'No—please,' protested Edmund with a quiet dignity. 'I cannot let you do this for me. God has prepared me to face death. I am reconciled to my fate.'

'You, maybe,' replied Blake with a saturnine twist to his lips, 'but not so your sister. 'Tis I who will have to face her wrath should I fail to get you out of this place.'

'Katherine?' said Edmund with some surprise. 'But I would have thought her to be the gentlest of women.'

'Ha!' exclaimed Blake, struggling with his buttons. 'The wench is wilful, troublesome and quarrelsome, I'll have you know.'

Edmund gave him an amused sidelong look. 'And yet you will marry her? Then it seems that life will not be dull for you.'

'Aye—that's true,' grinned Blake. 'I love her and would not have her any other way. When I learn how to handle her correctly I promise you that she will coo like a turtle dove. Here,' he said, handing Edmund his jacket, breeches and boots, standing in nothing but his hose. 'You're almost my height not as broad but the cape will conceal that.'

Feeling there was little to be gained in further protestation, that Blake would not be swayed from this plan of escape, Edmund began pulling on the scarlet suit, and as if by magic Jack produced some soot, rubbing it into Edmund's fair locks before covering them with the wide-brimmed hat. Standing back, Blake surveyed their handiwork, nodding with approval.

'You'll do,' he said. 'The turnkey didn't take a good look at my features but remember to keep your face in shadow in any case. The Master Keeper is a different matter so steer clear of him. A carriage will be waiting outside the prison to take you to the docks where a ship, the *Western Star*, is due to leave for the Indies. The captain has instructions to put in at a port on the French coast.'

'And you? How will you explain this?'

'Don't worry. It is all taken care of. A good blow to the chin—given me by Jack, here, should render me senseless for a while. By the time the alarm is raised by my coachman waiting outside—when I am discovered robbed of my clothes and knocked out— and you are nowhere to be found—then it will be assumed that you are responsible—that you saw a chance to escape and took it. By that time—please God, you will be far away from here, ready to sail with the tide.'

Edmund's features were suffused with emotion and he swallowed hard. 'How can I ever thank you enough?'

'I do not wish for gratitude,' said Blake gravely. 'It will be enough to see the joy on your sister's face when she knows you are safe across the water in France. She will be at the docks waiting to bid you farewell.'

'You are a fine man, Lord Russell. How I wish

that things could have been otherwise—that I had been allowed the chance to know you better. My sister is indeed fortunate.'

'Then let us pray that we will meet again in better times.'

Leaving Blake senseless on the cell floor, Father Edmund's escape from Newgate gaol was ridiculously easy and uneventful, but the lack of opposition owing to the turnkey's curiosity to watch the condemned felons leave for Tyburn under a heavy barrage of missiles being thrown by the crowd, and the complete unexpectedness of it, made it understandable.

The turnkey who had escorted Lord Russell inside the prison returned to escort him out, seeing nothing different about his person to make him suspect he was any other than the gentleman he had shown in earlier. Clad in Blake's clothes Father Edmund, keeping his face in shadow beneath the wide brim of his hat, passed through the prison gates and walked towards the waiting carriage and climbed inside. The coach driver whipped up the horses and headed off in the direction of the docks.

The docks were congested that day as Katherine waited for her brother, the air rent with the harsh cry of seagulls. The wharves and warehouses, built during the reign of Queen Elizabeth, crammed both sides of the Pool of London, serving not only quayside traffic but also the bigger ships that were unloaded in midstream. Cargoes which had been discharged from ships and cleared by customs were piled up and there was a strong smell, a mixture of boiling tar and rotting fish.

For Katherine, sitting inside the coach on this crucial day with Amelia, the agony of waiting for Edmund to arrive was almost intolerable. Before she had come to the docks she had been buoyed up with the hope that everything would go as planned, but now the waiting was beginning to get to her. What if everything had gone disastrously wrong and Blake had been arrested? What if they both should hang? Haunted by these terrible apprehensions, she gripped Amelia's hand.

'Oh, Amelia—why doesn't he come? What can have happened?'

Amelia, equally as tense for she was anxious about her own brother's safety, patted her hand comfortingly. 'Calm yourself, Katherine. We are early. I'm sure everything will be all right. Blake is aware of the risks involved and will take the utmost care.'

With this Katherine was obliged to be content, but as she continued to wait she felt as if she were suspended in time as she nervously twisted her handkerchief in her trembling fingers. The tide was high and her eyes sought out the *Western Star* among the many colourful ships at anchor on the river, where great activity was taking place as seamen scrubbed and swilled decks, repairing broken seams and canvas sailcloth. The *Western Star* was ready to weigh anchor in midstream as soon as its expected passenger climbed on board. A boat with an oarsman waited at the quayside to row him out to the great ship with its gilded hull and tall skeletal masts.

At long last a coach came careering onto the wharf and Katherine knew at once that it carried her brother, but terror, fear, doubt, all these feelings she had experienced in the past hour, rendered her numb. At length she gasped, 'I must go to him.'

'No—Katherine, wait,' but Amelia let her go, knowing it was useless to try and restrain her until he had alighted from the carriage. She watched, transfixed, as Katherine flew across the ground that separated them and tumbled into her brother's arms as he stepped down onto the wharf, although Amelia scarcely recognised him as the sombre priest, dressed as he was in Blake's scarlet suit and his fair hair blackened with soot.

At first Katherine was too deeply moved and happy for speech. At last they drew apart.

'Thank God you are safe,' she gasped, and then she asked the question uppermost in her mind, searching her brother's eyes for confirmation. 'Blake? Is—is he all right?'

'I am certain he will be. I told him it was foolhardy to attempt such a thing, but he would not listen.'

'That's just like him. Is he still inside the prison?'

'Yes, but when they find him they will release him. Fear not, Katherine,' he said, seeing the fear cloud her eyes, 'there is nothing to connect him with me.

It will be thought that he was set upon by me when he left Jack Nolan to find his own way out of the prison. I shall be eternally grateful to him. He is a good man—indeed, one of the finest men it has been my privilege to meet. He was prepared to lay down his life for me, Katherine. No man could ask for more.'

'Did—did he tell you that we are to be married?'

'Yes, he did, and I wish you every joy and happiness together. Before I go I have something to give you.'

Katherine watched as he removed a plain gold ring from his finger and, taking her hand, he placed it on the middle finger of her right hand. He was visibly moved as he raised it and pressed it to his lips, looking down into her eyes bright with unshed tears.

'This was our mother's ring, Katherine. The ring your father gave to her on their wedding day. It was her dearest wish, just before she died, that if we should chance to meet I should give it to you.'

Katherine stared down at it, feeling a hard choking lump rise in the back of her throat. Her heart swelled with a great wave of tenderness and love for her mother, who she had never known but who had thought of her daughter in her last hour.

'Thank you, Edmund. I shall treasure it always.'

Her heart was heavy within her that her brother should leave her so soon after finding her. She would have clung to him, reluctant to let him go but, aware of the impatience of the boatman waiting to row him out to the ship, and the danger to them both if they lingered too long, he cut their farewell short. Taking both her hands in his own, he drew them to his lips, kissing them gently.

'Farewell, Katherine. We have only known each other for a short while but I feel as if I had known you for a lifetime. And—who knows, when times are less troubled, one day I might find myself knocking on your door at Ludgrove Hall. I will write to you from France before going on to Rome—I promise.'

He smiled at her in his tender way, wiping away an unhappy tear which trailed slowly down her pale cheek, which betrayed her inner sadness. 'Don't weep, Katherine. Be happy, for you, my dear, dear sister, have everything to live for,' and with those final words he bent and brushed her cheek with his lips before turning from her and striding towards the boat.

Katherine watched until the boat had reached the *Western Star* and Edmund had climbed the ladder thrown over its side. She saw his tall figure being greeted on deck by the captain, and before he disappeared from her sight he turned and looked towards where she stood on the wharf and raised his arm in a gesture of farewell.

Before Katherine left the wharf, the *Western Star* was already on its way, dipping gracefully in the choppy waters as it manoeuvred its way between other ships, heading out to sea.

* * *

Katherine's wait at the docks for her brother to arrive safe from the bowels of Newgate gaol had been intolerable, but back at Landale House her wait for news of Blake had been doubly so. She had been incapable of sitting still for a moment, pacing the hall like a restless animal, her eyes fixed on the door leading to the street, her ears straining to the sounds of horses' hooves and carriages passing by outside, her hopes rising, her heart almost ceasing to beat, when she had thought they were stopping, only to sink back down into the dark depths of despair when they had carried on their way.

And then all of a sudden there he was, striding into the house with his easy gait, as casual and devil-may-care as if he were returning from a day with the hunt. Katherine's heart gave a joyful leap and for one blissful moment she let her eyes feast on his handsome features, on his skin, which still retained a hint of bronze from the tropical sun and wind, on his dark eyes and firm lips, crooked in a slow smile, his thick black hair tumbling untidily about his face.

This was the man she loved more than anything or anyone else in the whole world. That he wore the shabby clothes of a vagabond, which were the finest garments the prison could provide for his journey home without waiting for a fresh suit to be sent from Landale House, went unnoticed, for all Katherine could think of was that he was there. He was safe.

Tears were streaming down her cheeks, but they were the blessed tears of relief and gladness and she was carried along by an emotion of joy so strong it was almost madness.

'Blake,' she cried in a blaze of love.

He looked up and saw her flying across the hall towards him and then she was in his arms, laughing and crying at once, feeling herself caught in his strong grip.

As they came together they were unaware of anything around them, of Amelia and her husband stealing discreetly away—dispersing the inquisitive servants and leaving Blake and Katherine alone, cut off from the world by a storm of relief and passion that overwhelmed them. They stood pressed together in complete rapture as tears continued to flood Katherine's cheeks, washing away all the despair, the anxiety, which had gripped her all that day and which had seemed like an eternity. The minute Blake had walked through those doors had abolished all her suffering at one stroke.

Slowly Katherine calmed down, feeling a delicious feeling of security and well-being, given to her by the warmth and love of this man she adored above all else. She turned her face up to his.

'Oh, Blake—how I feared for you. You have no idea how much. The brutal images I conjured up in my mind—of what they would do to you should you be caught—passed all bounds of imagination.'

Blake put a gentle hand beneath her chin and looked deep into her eyes. 'Nothing is going to happen to me, my love. It's all over.' He bent and kissed her, cupping her face in his strong hands.

Only when he lifted his head did Katherine notice the faint purple bruise on his chin. Reaching up, she touched it gently with the tips of her fingers, her eyes enquiring. He grinned.

'Jack Nolan gave me that. It added credence to my story. So convincing was my anger—that I had been knocked senseless by an inmate while making my own way out of the prison—the turnkey having failed to turn up on time to escort me, owing to the fact that he was too absorbed in watching the condemned felons being carted off to Tyburn—that the keeper was quite beside himself. After almost suffering a seizure upon discovering the priest had escaped, he became a deperate bumbling fool—no doubt worried that he will be replaced—and was full of apologies at the dastardly treatment I had experienced inside the gaol. He had no reason to associate me with Father Edmund in the slightest. As far as they are concerned, he saw a chance to escape and took it. Needless to say, a desperate search is under way to recapture him. Did you see him at the docks?'

'Yes. He'll be halfway to France by now.' Once again Katherine melted into his arms. 'I cannot thank you enough for all you have done, Blake. Without you he would never have got out of that place—only on the day of his execution.' She tilted her head and looked up at him, her eyes filled with brilliance. 'You are a truly remarkable man, Lord Russell.'

'No—not remarkable,' he amended. 'Lucky, I would say. Lucky that I have you.'

Carried away by the touch of her, the scent of her hair, feeling her slender form pressed close, Blake realised he was in danger of letting his fiercely burning desire get the better of him, and in another moment he would swing her up into his arms and carry her up to his chamber and make love to her. Gently he pushed her away and Katherine's heart soared at the desire she saw glowing in his dark eyes. Tenderly he took her hand and kissed her palm, and then, resting his hands on her shoulders, he looked deep into her eyes.

'We must take care, my love,' he said huskily, 'else there is a strong probability that I shall make you mine before we have taken our vows.' He sighed deeply, brushing a heavy lock of dark hair from his face. 'I am heartily tired of London. Tomorrow we shall leave for Ludgrove Hall. There we shall be married as soon as it can be arranged. Then you will be mine, Katherine—flesh of my flesh—wholly and completely. How will that please you?'

'Yes,' she whispered. 'I can think of nothing that would please me more.'

'And your aunt? How do you think she will react to the news that you are to be my wife?'

Katherine frowned. The spell was broken. Abruptly she turned from him, struggling against this looming menace which had invaded her peace, for indeed this was one obstacle she had not considered.

'My aunt! In all truth there has been so much happening of late that I have not given her a moment's thought. I have a distinct feeling that she will set herself against the match. When she sent me to London to look for a husband she wanted me out of her life for good. She will not take kindly to my returning to be the next Lady Russell. She will never accept it.'

Blake turned her round and caught her up in his arms fiercely. 'Frankly, Katherine, I care not one way or the other what your aunt thinks. She cannot stop us marrying. If she cannot accept you as my wife then she will have to retire to the Dower house. I love you deeply, Katherine, and I mean for us to be happy together at Ludgrove Hall. I will not allow your aunt, or anyone else for that matter, to spoil our happiness. So—you can set your mind at rest.'

Katherine and Blake were married at Appleby church at a time when new trials and dangers beset the nation. News came to them at Ludgrove Hall that trained bands of volunteers in London had taken up arms in defence of the liberty of the Commons. There, the friends of the King, in fear for their lives, fled. The Queen had secretly left England, nominally to visit her daughter in Holland, but in reality to pawn Crown jewels with which to buy arms. The King had left London and had begun summoning all loyal subjects to his aid. Already the country was divided into two great parties—King and Parliament.

Lord Forbes still languished in the Tower awaiting trial, when he would be found guilty of his crime and given a further few months' imprisonment before being released. Out of favour with the Court, he would return to his home in Hereford before taking up the call to arms and going to join the King.

To Katherine and Blake on their wedding day all this was set aside. Katherine had been right when she had told Blake that her aunt would never accept her as his wife. When she saw they were determined on this she moved to the Dower house, which was in close proximity to Ludgrove Hall, of her own accord, although she did attend the wedding and, as time went by, she slowly mellowed towards the situation. As expected, Matilda, with her own wedding to a wealthy, personable young man looming close, was delighted with the whole affair.

In Appleby the nuptial bells peeled out for their wedding which was a truly grand affair. Guests began arriving at Ludgrove Hall the day before and the whole village turned out in its Sunday best to watch the brilliant procession which made its way to the church and then back to Ludgrove Hall. Katherine had never thought she could be so happy, and as a bride in her ivory silk gown she was by far the loveliest lady of them all. A magnificent banquet had been laid in the great hall at Ludgrove Hall where

Blake and Katherine held centre stage, while secretly longing to be gone from all these people and to be alone together.

It was late when they reached their chamber and it was not until the servants had been dismissed and they lay together on the huge four-poster bed, with firelight caressing their bodies, that they came together, naked and unashamed. The ecstasy of their union, the sweet agony of their passion, was a joy undreamed of which, even when they drew apart, remained unslaked. Blake deliberately and artfully awoke passions in Katherine she hadn't known she possessed, turning her into a shameless, uninhibited wanton.

Only later, when they drew apart, did Blake smile and draw Katherine into the warm circle of his arms. Sighing with dreamy contentment Katherine placed her head on his chest, her glorious hair spread over them like a silken sheet.

'Do you hear it?' she whispered, her lips against his flesh, listening to the merrymaking of the guests still engaged in celebrating this memorable wedding. 'The guests are still celebrating. Were we selfish to leave when we did?'

'No. Tonight I want you all to myself, Katherine. Call that selfish if you like, my love, but to my mind every man and woman have the right to be alone on their wedding night.' He placed his lips against her hair. 'In fact, looking as ravishing as you did today, then 'tis a wonder I did not whisk you away sooner.'

He sighed deep with contentment, letting his head fall back onto the pillow. 'I ask for nothing more than to live a life of ease and contentment here at Ludgrove Hall with you, where, God willing, neither King nor Parliament can intrude.'

Katherine raised her head and looked at him, his words making her conscious of the one threat to their happiness. 'But what if it is true, Blake? That England faces civil war? What will you do?'

Blake's arms tightened about her as he looked towards the glowing embers of the fire. 'If it comes to that—as I fear it will, then I have a loyalty to the King. You cannot destroy something unless you have something constructive to replace it with. The alternative which Mr Pym and Mr Cromwell would foist on us is more far reaching than the transference of power from the King's hands into that of the High Court and Parliament. It fills me with dread.'

When Blake saw Katherine about to ask another question he put a finger to her lips, silencing her. 'Not now, Katherine. Now is not the time to speak of such matters. What will be will be, for nothing we can do or say will change that. But whatever comes, my one sure recompense is that I'll have you with me, always,' he murmured, lowering his head to hers and seeking her lips once more. 'But first we have our own happiness to think of—a future of our own which we will build together. So, now—my wilful—stubborn—wonderful wife, kiss me. The night is still young and I do not intend wasting one minute of it.'

Historical Romance

Coming next month

AN UNWILLING CONQUEST
Stephanie Laurens
REGENCY ENGLAND

Having seen his sister Lenore and brother Jack caught in Parson's mousetrap, albeit willingly, Harry Lester had *no* intention of following their example. Now the news was out that the Lester family fortunes had been repaired, Harry knew the matchmaking mamas would be in pursuit, so he promptly left London for Newmarket, only to find himself acting as the rescuer of Mrs Lucinda Babbacombe, a beautiful *managing* widow, who refused to accept his advice! No matter that he desired her—marriage was out!

THE COMTE AND THE COURTESAN
Truda Taylor
FRANCE 1789

After ten years in Paris under the protection of the elderly Marquis Philippe de Maupilier, Madeleine Vaubonne was well aware that she was mistakenly thought to be his mistress. Even so, it was a nasty surprise when Lucian de Valori, the Comte de Regnay, offered to replace Philippe in her bed! She forcefully refused his proposition, but when Philippe died Lucian was the only one to offer help. Reluctantly she agreed to his escort to her home in Brittany, the start of a journey neither had expected to make…